No Ordinary Sound

Sound

A Melody Classic
Volume 1

by Denise Lewis Patrick

★ American Girl®

Published by American Girl Publishing

16 17 18 19 20 21 22 LEO 10 9 8 7 6 5 4 3 2 1

Cover image by Michael Dwornik and Juliana Kolesova
Cover photo of crowd reflection © Bob Adelman/Corbis
Author photo by Fran Baltzer Photo

Cataloging-in-Publication Data available from the Library of Congress

To everyone who hears the call of justice, and answers.

Beforever™

The adventurous characters you'll meet in
the BeForever books will spark your curiosity
about the past, inspire you to find your voice
in the present, and excite you about your future.
You'll make friends with these girls as you share
their fun and their challenges. Like you, they are
bright and brave, imaginative and energetic,
creative and kind. Just as you are, they are
discovering what really matters: Helping others.
Being a true friend. Protecting the earth.
Standing up for what's right. Read their stories,
explore their worlds, join their adventures.
Your friendship with them will BeForever.

♪ TABLE *of* CONTENTS ♪

When Melody's story takes place, the terms "Negro," "colored," and "black" were all used to describe Americans of African descent. You'll see all of those words used in this book.

Today, "Negro" and "colored" can be offensive because they are associated with racial inequality. "African American" is a more contemporary term, but it wasn't commonly used until the late 1980s.

Meet the Ellisons

It was a perfect day in May, and Melody Ellison could hardly wait for her father to pull the car to a stop in front of her grandparents' house. Every Sunday, Melody and her family had dinner here after church. But today was different. Melody was almost bursting with news. She hopped out of the station wagon so quickly that she forgot to hold the door for her sister Lila, who was coming out behind her.

"Hey!" Lila shouted, but nine-year-old Melody was already halfway up the front walk. She only slowed to look at the purple petunias clustered near the steps. Then she skipped up to the front porch and peered into the big front windows. She could hear music coming from inside, and couldn't help tapping her shiny shoes. Music always made her want to *move*.

"What are you so hot after?" asked Dwayne, Melody's older brother. His long legs had brought him around the car and up behind her in only a few steps.

"I'm not hot," Melody answered, before she realized that Dwayne was joking. He only meant that she was excited, and she was. She couldn't hold her surprise in any longer.

"Miss Dorothy asked me to sing a solo for Youth Day," she said proudly. Youth Day was far away in October, but it was the biggest children's program at their church. Kids from all over the city came to sing, play music, recite poetry, and even perform in skits. Only a few kids got the chance to stand in front to sing solo parts, and they had to be very, very good.

Dwayne raised his eyebrows, and Melody watched his face nervously. It wasn't easy to impress him. Dwayne was eighteen, and he'd done his first solo when he was eight.

"Wow, congratulations!" he said. "You've gotta write Yvonne and tell her."

Melody grinned. Yvonne was their oldest sister, who was away at college. She was a good singer too. In fact, all the members of Melody's family were musical.

"I will," she promised. "As soon as we get home."

"Tell Yvonne what?" Lila joined them, trying to balance a plate with their mother's foil-wrapped triple-chocolate cake and push her eyeglasses up on her nose at the same time.

"Melody's going to be the star of the New Hope Baptist Church Youth Day," he said, grabbing the plate as it wobbled. "Just like I'm going to be the biggest Motown star since Smokey Robinson."

"I don't know," Lila sniffed matter-of-factly, and nodded toward Melody. "Dee-Dee might beat you to it." Lila was thirteen, and sometimes acted like she knew everything in the world.

"Not me." Melody shook her head. She liked to pretend she was a singing star at home, using her hairbrush as a microphone. But she didn't like to be in the spotlight. She felt safe from her spot in the children's choir when the congregation was full of the church family she'd known all her life. But she was nervous about standing alone on Youth Day, in front of a big crowd full of faces she didn't know.

Melody's parents crowded onto the porch. The delicious aroma of Big Momma's pot roast and gravy wafted outside. "Boy, that sure smells good, doesn't it?" Melody's father whispered.

Melody's tummy answered with a gurgle, and she nodded.

Melody's mother laughed. "Will, you always did think my mother was the best cook in the world."

"Well, she is, Frances!" Mr. Ellison said, loosening his tie.

"Did anybody ring the doorbell?" Lila asked.

Melody shook her head and reached out to push the bell. Just then, Big Momma swung open the door.

Melody had always thought it was funny that they called her grandmother Big Momma, since she wasn't much taller than Melody. But the name was a sign of respect. Besides, when her grandmother sang, her voice was very big.

"Hello, my chicks!" Big Momma said. She greeted each of her grandchildren with a rose-scented squeeze.

"Big Momma, this is Detroit, Michigan. You left all your chickens back in Alabama, remember?" Dwayne said, ducking out of her arms.

Melody lingered a little longer, until Lila nudged her to get a turn. But when Lila strolled over to check

out the latest magazines on the coffee table, Big
Momma folded her arms and gave Melody a stern look.
"I believe you've got something to tell me," she said.

"Yes!" Melody exclaimed. "Miss Dorothy asked
me to learn a solo over the summer for the Youth Day
pro—" She stopped. Big Momma was smiling and
nodding. Melody stared at her grandmother in wonder.
"You already knew!" Melody said. "How?"

"Are you kidding?" Lila said from the sofa. "Big
Momma and Miss Dorothy are best friends. They tell
each other everything. They were in a gospel singing
group together before we were even born."

Big Momma laughed. "Yes, Dorothy and I trained
to be music teachers together back in Alabama, and we
traveled around singing in churches. She says you're
ready to carry a song on your own."

"Who is ready for what?" Melody's mother asked
from the dining room.

"Melody's doing a Youth Day solo," Lila told her.

"Oh, that's wonderful, honey!" Mrs. Ellison clapped
her hands and rushed to give Melody a hug.

"Thanks, Mommy," Melody said, suddenly feeling
shy at all the attention.

"I believe our Melody is ready to sing out," Mr. Ellison said, as he placed extra chairs at the dining table. Melody heard the pride in his voice and wished she felt as confident as he did. She tugged at the end of her braid.

Big Momma put her arm around Melody's shoulders. "It's okay to be nervous, baby chick," she said, reading Melody's mind. "You have all summer to practice. I'll help."

"But what about your students?" Melody asked. Big Momma taught piano and voice lessons to kids and grown-ups, right in her living room.

"Don't worry, I'll find the time."

"Thanks, Big Momma." Melody felt her nerves flutter again. But she felt good knowing that her family believed so much in her. She skipped into the dining room, where Lila was setting the blue plates onto the yellow-checked tablecloth.

"Remember," Melody's mother said, handing Melody a stack of paper napkins. "We've been a musical family for generations."

"See? I *knew* I was born to be a big name in the music business!" Dwayne said. He did a quick spinning dance move before he set a basket of rolls on the table.

Melody laughed as she carefully folded each napkin into a triangle and tucked one beside every plate.

"You're so silly!" Lila said to him, shaking her head.

"The thing about Youth Day is that I get to pick my own song," Melody told her brother. "But I don't know which one to sing."

"We could try some songs after dinner." Dwayne winked at Melody. She knew he took every chance he could to play Big Momma's beloved piano.

"*After* dinner means we need to *eat* dinner first, doesn't it?" Melody's father said.

"But we can't start without Poppa," Dwayne said.

Melody looked up from the napkins. Where was her grandfather, anyway, she wondered, turning to Big Momma.

Big Momma shrugged, but Melody saw a twinkle in her eyes. Before Melody could ask anything, she heard the back door of the house open and shut. Poppa's heavy footsteps crossed the floor.

"Hello!" his voice boomed. Poppa always talked loud. Melody's mother said it was because of his work around all the loud machines years ago at the auto factory. Melody liked the sound—it reminded her of drumbeats.

"Guess who I brought to dinner!" Poppa called from the kitchen.

Everyone turned in his direction. He opened the door wider, and there stood Yvonne with a huge smile on her face.

"Surprise!" she sang.

"Vonnie!" Melody ran around the table to give her big sister a hug.

"We didn't expect you till next week!" Mrs. Ellison said. Melody could tell that her mother was very happy. Yvonne had been gone since January.

"I took all my exams and I finished my last paper early, so I caught the bus," Yvonne explained. "Poppa picked me up at the Detroit terminal. Boy, that ride from Alabama takes forever!" She barely took a breath before dropping her bag and greeting everyone. "Wow, Dee-Dee. Did you get taller? Got any new sounds, Dwayne? Lila, are those new glasses? Dad, you're wearing the birthday shirt we gave you! Big Momma, that roast smells really good. And Mommy, I know you made your triple-chocolate cake. Can we eat?"

Melody laughed. College hadn't changed Yvonne's habit of talking a mile a minute.

Big Momma brought the roast in and everyone took their places around the table, with Poppa at one end and Daddy at the other. And now the family was truly all together, the way their Sundays used to be.

"Dee-Dee, why don't you sing grace for us?" her father said.

"Yes, Daddy," Melody said. She felt comfortable singing in front of *this* crowd. She bowed her head and sang in a strong, clear voice:

> *By Thy hands must we be fed;*
> *Give us, Lord, our daily bread.*

Table Talk

o," Yvonne said, "what's the news? What have I been missing?" She glanced around the table.

"I'm doing double shifts at the factory again this week," Daddy told her.

Melody opened her mouth to speak, but Mommy beat her to it.

"There's a lot of talk about some of the city schools only having half days next year," she said.

Everyone looked up at that. "Really?" Yvonne asked.

Mommy nodded. "Can you believe that? School three or four hours a day? Children need as much time as they can get to learn. We teachers are against it, but the district says there may not be enough money for full days."

"Wish they'd shortened the days when I was in school!" Dwayne grunted.

"I have news . . ." Melody started to say. But Yvonne nodded in Dwayne's direction.

"What's up with you?" she asked him.

"Not much," Dwayne said, leaning over his almost empty plate.

Melody looked at him curiously. When he wasn't working at the factory, Dwayne was always busy singing with his friends or writing new music—and playing Big Momma's piano every chance he could get. Why would he tell Yvonne "not much"? She wanted to ask him, but she also wanted her turn.

Melody waved her fork in the air at her sister, trying not to see Mommy frowning at her poor table manners. "Vonnie, I was going to write you, but now I can tell you in person."

"Spill it, Dee-Dee!" Yvonne laughed.

"I'm going to sing my first solo!"

"In the Mother's Day program next week?" Yvonne asked.

"No, Miss Dorothy picked me for the Youth Day program. I have the whole summer to learn a song."

"That's great!" Yvonne said. "Now you can show that girl—what's her name? The one who always tries to boss the other singers around?"

"You mean Diane Harris?" Melody made a face. Diane was in the same fourth-grade class as Melody and took piano lessons from Big Momma. She had a nice voice, but she wasn't at all nice about that.

"I hear she's a solo hog," Dwayne mumbled with his mouth full.

"We can't be jealous of other people's gifts," Mommy said to Dwayne sternly. She turned to Melody. "Besides, didn't you just say that Miss Dorothy asked *you* to sing a solo?"

"Yes." Melody looked down, twiddling her fingers in her lap. "But I'm really not as good as Diane."

"Who says that?" Daddy asked.

Melody said out loud what she'd been thinking since Miss Dorothy's request. "Well, Diane has a big, grown-up voice, and I only have a girl voice." She looked at Dwayne, expecting him to remind her that she *was* only a girl. He didn't say anything.

"Everybody's got a right to shine, baby chick," Big Momma said. "Diane does and you do, too.

You've got a beautiful voice, and plenty of other gifts."

"What about that green thumb of yours?" Poppa reminded her.

Lila said, "I bet Diane can't name every car off the Ford line, the way you can!"

Melody smiled. It was true that she was good at all those things. And she liked being good at them, too. But Diane was so sure of herself when she sang! She could hear a song once and sing it without one mistake. Melody remembered music easily, but she had to practice and practice to get the words right.

"You're a hard worker, Melody. That's a gift, too," Mommy said, and then turned to Yvonne. "Speaking of hard work, how was your second year at Tuskegee?"

"Yes, Vonnie. Did you study all the time?" Melody asked. Mommy had gone to Tuskegee, and this year Dwayne had applied and been accepted. Melody knew that her parents hoped all their children would graduate from Tuskegee one day, too.

Yvonne shook her head so that her small earrings sparkled. "There's so much more to do at school besides studying," she said, reaching for more gravy.

"Like what?" Poppa asked, propping his elbows on the table. Melody held back a giggle when she saw Big Momma frown the same way Mommy had, but Poppa paid no attention.

"Well, last week before finals a bunch of us went out to help black people in the community register to vote," Yvonne said. "And do you know, a lady told me she was too afraid to sign up."

"Why was she afraid?" Melody interrupted.

"Because somebody threw a rock through her next-door neighbor's window after her neighbor voted," Yvonne explained, her eyes flashing with anger. "This is 1963! How can anybody get away with that?"

Melody looked from Yvonne to her father. "You always say not voting is like not being able to talk. Why wouldn't anybody want to talk?"

Daddy sighed. "It's not that she doesn't want to vote, Melody. There are a lot of unfair rules down South that keep our people from exercising their rights. Some white people will do anything, including scaring black people, to keep change from happening. They don't want to share jobs or neighborhoods or schools with us. Voting is like a man or woman's voice speaking out to change those laws and rules."

"And it's not just about voting," Mommy said. "Remember what Rosa Parks did in Montgomery? She stood up for her rights."

"You mean she *sat down* for her rights," Melody said. Melody knew all about Mrs. Parks, who got arrested for simply sitting down on a city bus. She had paid her fare like everybody else, but because she was a Negro the bus driver told her she had to give her seat to a white person! *But that happened eight years ago,* Melody realized. *Why haven't things changed?*

"Aren't we just as good as anybody else?" Melody asked as she looked around the table. "The laws should be fair everywhere, for everybody, right?"

"That's not always the way life works," Poppa said.

"Why not?" Lila asked.

Poppa sat back and rubbed his silvery mustache. That always meant he was about to tell a story.

"Back in Alabama, there was a white farmer who owned the land next to ours. Palmer was his name. Decent fellow. We went into town the same day to sell our peanut crops. It wasn't a good growing year, but I'd lucked out with twice as many sacks of peanuts as

Palmer. Well, at the market they counted and weighed his sacks. Then they counted and weighed my sacks. Somehow Palmer got twice as much money as I got for selling half the crop I had. They never even checked the quality of what we had, either."

"What?" Lila blurted out.

"How?" Melody scooted to the edge of her chair.

"Wait, now." Poppa waved his grandchildren quiet. "I asked the man to weigh it again, but he refused. I complained. Even Palmer spoke up for me. But that man turned to me and said, 'Boy—'"

"He called you *boy*?" Dwayne interrupted, putting his fork down.

"'Boy,'" Poppa continued, "'this is all you're gonna get. And if you keep up this trouble, you won't have any farm to go back to!'"

Melody's mouth fell open. "What was he talking about? You did have a farm," she said, glancing at Big Momma.

"He meant we were in danger of losing our farm— our home—because your grandfather spoke out to a white man," Big Momma explained. She shook her head slowly. "As hard as we'd worked to buy that land, as hard as it was for colored people to own anything in Alabama, we decided that day that we had to sell and move north."

Although Melody had heard many of her grandfather's stories about life in Alabama before, she'd never heard this one. And as she considered it, she realized that on their many trips down South, she'd never seen the old family farm. Maybe her grandparents didn't want to go back.

Melody sighed. Maybe the lady Yvonne mentioned didn't want to risk losing *her* home if she "spoke out" by voting. But Yvonne was right—it was hard to understand how that could happen in the United States of America in 1963!

Poppa was shaking his head. "It's a shame that colored people today still have to be afraid of standing up or speaking out for themselves."

"Negroes," Mommy corrected him.

"Black people," Yvonne said firmly.

"Well, what *are* we supposed to call ourselves?" Lila asked.

Melody thought about how her grandparents usually said "colored." They were older and from the

South, and Big Momma said that's what was proper when they were growing up. Mommy and Daddy mostly said "Negroes." But ever since she went to college, Yvonne was saying "black people." Melody noticed that Mommy and Daddy were saying it sometimes, too. She liked the way it went with "white people," like a matched set. But sometimes she wished they didn't need all these color words at all. Melody spoke up. "What about 'Americans'?" she said.

Yvonne still seemed upset. "That's right, Dee-Dee. We're Americans. We have the same rights as white Americans. There shouldn't be any separate water fountains or waiting rooms or public bathrooms. Black Americans deserve equal treatment and equal pay. And sometimes we have to remind people."

"How do we remind them?" Lila asked. Melody was wondering the same thing.

"By not shopping at stores that won't hire black workers," Yvonne explained. "By picketing in front of a restaurant that won't serve black people. By marching."

"You won't catch me protesting or picketing or marching in any street," Dwayne interrupted, working on his third helping of potatoes. "I'm gonna be onstage or in the recording studio, making music and getting famous."

Mr. Ellison shook his head, and Melody knew there was going to be another argument, the way there always was when Dwayne talked about becoming a music star.

"Don't forget," Daddy said, "when you graduated high school early, we agreed that you'd work in the factory until the summer was over, and then go on to college. I couldn't go to college, and now I'm working double shifts at a factory so you can! You could *study* music in college!"

Mommy was nodding. Melody knew that her parents were disappointed whenever Dwayne talked about skipping college. She saw Dwayne stop eating to look down at his plate—not at his father—and she felt bad for her brother. Melody hated when they argued. So when her brother looked as if he might say something, Melody interrupted.

"Daddy," Melody said. "Dwayne can sing and write music already, and he can play the piano almost as good as Big Momma can. He's really talented. It's like Big Momma says—everybody's got a right to shine."

Daddy smiled at Melody. "I hope your brother is smart enough to appreciate it when you girls stick up for him," he said. "But with a college degree, your brother would have a whole lot of opportunities."

"Let's save this talk for later," Mommy said.

Melody blew out a relieved breath. She didn't want their great day to be ruined by a disagreement.

"I say everybody needs to cool down with some ice cream and cake," Big Momma said. She got up and headed for the kitchen.

Dwayne escaped to the living room. Yvonne stayed at the table, talking to their father and grandfather about her plans for a summer job. Melody gathered the salt and pepper shakers, which were shaped like two fat penguins, got up, and put them away.

A soft, slow tune was coming from Big Momma's piano. Dwayne was playing, making up a new song. Melody listened for him to sing some words, but there weren't any. Maybe he hadn't thought of them yet. She wandered to the archway between the rooms just as the phone beside the sofa rang.

"Children, answer that for me!" Big Momma called from the kitchen.

Melody started into the living room, but Dwayne had already grabbed the big black telephone receiver without noticing her.

"Hello!" Dwayne answered breathlessly. And then, instead of calling either of his grandparents or taking a message, he lowered his voice.

"Yeah?" he almost whispered. "Make it quick. I told you this is my grandfather's number. Okay. I'm working on the song now. I'll meet you later."

"Who is it?" Poppa asked from the table. Dwayne dropped the receiver into the cradle with a clatter.

"Are you getting calls from your girlfriends on my telephone?" Poppa laughed. So did Daddy and Yvonne.

"No, sir," Dwayne called quickly. His eyes met Melody's. He had a funny expression on his face. She'd heard him talking to girls on the phone before, and that wasn't how he'd sounded. Dwayne definitely had a secret.

"Was that about your singing group?" she asked.

Dwayne pulled her farther into the living room. "Yeah, but after that scrape with Dad, I'd rather not announce this, okay? That was Artie's brother. He just got hired as a musician at Motown, and he's gonna try to get us an audition." Artie was Dwayne's buddy and a member of his singing group, The Detroiters.

"That's so exciting, Dwayne!" Melody exclaimed.

"Shhh," Dwayne insisted. "Can you keep it a secret?"

Melody pinched her finger and thumb together and slid them across her lips, as if she were closing a zipper. That was the signal she and her brother and sisters used with one another, meaning, "I won't tell anyone!"

Dwayne's shoulders relaxed, and he went back to the piano. Melody followed.

Dwayne held his hands dramatically over the piano keys. "How about you singing this for your Youth Day solo?" he said, beginning to play and sing something different—and lively. *Grandpa Poppa had a farm . . . "*

Melody giggled, shaking her head at how he'd changed the words of the old kindergarten rhyme. From all around the house, her family joined in:

"E-i-e-i-ohhhh!"

Let Your Light Shine

♪ CHAPTER 3 ♪

The next morning, Melody and Lila left home together to walk to school. Lila's junior high was only two blocks away from Melody's elementary school. As usual, they had trouble untangling Bojangles, their small mixed terrier, from their legs when they got to the front door. Lila took Bo's red ball from the bag hanging on the coat tree and tossed it. And as usual, he fell for the trick and went scampering after the ball. The girls hurried out.

At the corner, they paused to wait for Melody's best friend, Sharon. Sharon lived three blocks up the street, and Melody always watched to see her front gate swing open as Sharon ran to meet them. Sharon always ran.

"Hey!" Sharon waved as her strong legs flew along the sidewalk.

Melody was eager to see if Sharon had remembered

that it was "Matching Monday," and had worn red hair ribbons as they'd planned. "You didn't forget!" Melody said.

"'Course not," Sharon said, turning her head so Melody could admire the crisply ironed satin ribbons that were tied in neat bows at the tops of her two pigtails.

"Nice." Melody nodded and checked quickly to see if her own red ribbons were still tied tightly. They were.

"So, are you super excited about Youth Day?" Sharon asked. They were both in the children's choir. "What are you going to sing?"

"I don't know yet," Melody answered.

"Does it have to be a church song?"

Melody hadn't considered that question. Both girls looked at Lila, who was walking and reading a book at the same time.

"Lila, Mommy told you to stop doing that," Melody reminded her sister.

"Yeah," Sharon chimed in. "Didn't you run right into a light post one time while you were reading?"

Lila glared at them. She slapped her book closed and promptly dropped it. Melody picked it up.

"Anyway," Melody continued, "did you hear Sharon? About the song?"

"Yes," Lila said. "And of course it has to be a church song, sillies. It's a program at the church!"

Melody hadn't said a word about Dwayne's secret to her sisters or even to Sharon. But the tune that he had been playing on Big Momma's piano snuck into Melody's head during her morning math class, and stayed there through her spelling quiz. At lunchtime, she tapped her milk carton to the rhythm while Sharon and a boy named Julius argued about the Detroit Tigers baseball team.

By the time she and Sharon lined up for dodgeball in gym that afternoon, Melody was humming her brother's nameless, wordless tune out loud. A high-pitched voice spoke behind her.

"What's *that* song?" It was Diane Harris.

Melody glanced at Sharon. They always thought it was interesting that Diane's speaking voice was high and screechy, but that when she opened her mouth to sing, such a smooth sound came out.

"Just music in my head," Melody said. She wouldn't give away anything about Dwayne's new creation.

"Well, I've never heard it before," Diane said, as if she'd heard all the music in the entire world. She blew a big bubble-gum bubble, and popped it.

Melody took a deep breath, thinking of what Big Momma had said about letting other people shine. "I guess you're one of the first, then," Melody said.

"Harris!" the gym teacher shouted. "Gum in the trash can! Ellison, you lead Team One."

Melody smiled and stepped forward. She wasn't very good at sports, so whenever she got a chance to make up a team, she tried to pick some kids who were good and some who weren't. Julius was chosen as captain of Team Two. He picked Sharon before Melody could. It was no surprise that Diane was the last to be picked. It wasn't that she was a bad player—she was just so bossy! She always seemed to think *she* was the team captain.

"Okay, Harris," the teacher called. "You're on Team One. Let's go!"

Diane waved Melody over. "I'll tell you how to position everybody," she said as the class trailed out to the playground. "Our team is pretty weak except for me, so—"

Before Diane could finish, Melody thought of something Mommy always said when things didn't quite go the way she'd planned. "That's okay," Melody said cheerfully. "We'll make it work."

The game was fierce and fun. The score was tied just before the bell rang. Diane sent the ball flying in Team Two's direction. Julius dodged it. Sharon jumped up to catch it. All at once the ball was sailing back. Melody jumped up, but it bounced right off her fingers.

"I got it!" Diane yelled, running from the back of the field. She spiked the ball back. Then the bell sounded, and most of the kids ran for the school building.

"See, I should have been in front because I'm taller," Diane grumbled. "It was a lucky win."

"It's a win just the same, right?" Melody smiled at her as Sharon jogged up to them. Diane walked on by without saying anything.

"Right," Sharon whispered, before the girls went inside arm in arm.

♬

After school, Melody said good-bye to Sharon at her corner. "See you at choir rehearsal!" she called as she raced ahead of Lila. Melody was hoping that Yvonne was home and that the three sisters could spend time together the way they used to before Yvonne went away to college. They ate cookies and combed one another's hair, and talked about anything that popped into their heads without Dwayne or their parents hearing. The "sister-thing" was what Yvonne called it.

"Why are you and Sharon always running?" Lila yelled after her. But Melody was already at the front door, pulling magazines and envelopes out of the mailbox.

"See? You had to wait for me anyway," Lila laughed, pulling out her heart-shaped key ring. Inside, Bo barked excitedly at the sound of their voices. Melody flipped through the mail in her hand. There was a small purple envelope in the bunch. She saw her own name written across the front in careful cursive handwriting.

"Oh! I got a letter from Val!" she said. Val was their

cousin who lived in Alabama. She was between Lila and Melody in age, and she was Melody's favorite playmate when they drove down to visit family every summer. Val and Melody had been pen pals since Melody was in second grade.

Lila looked interested. "What's she say this time?"

Melody ripped open the envelope as soon as she stepped inside and began reading out loud.

"Dear Dee-Dee. How are you and—"

"Skip that part," Lila said. She bent to pet Bo. He rolled onto his back and stuck his paws in the air.

"Okay. *You'll explode when you hear my news. We are moving to Detroit as soon as school is over!* What?" Melody screamed, forgetting all about the sister-thing. This news was even more surprising than Dwayne's secret.

Even Lila was surprised. "That's big!" she said. Bo sat up and barked in agreement.

"What's big?" Yvonne yawned, padding downstairs barefoot and still in pajamas.

Melody waved the letter in the air. "Val and her mom and dad are moving to Detroit!"

"That sure is news," Yvonne said. "I wonder what made Charles and Tish decide to move?"

"I don't know," Melody answered. "But I can't wait!"

"I think this calls for a celebration, don't you?" Yvonne asked.

"Yes!" Both Lila and Melody answered at once.

"Great." Yvonne rubbed her hands together. "Now, I think we need to start by raiding Dwayne's cookie stash."

Lila grinned. "They're hidden in the cupboard behind—"

"—the tuna fish!" Melody finished.

When Dwayne came home from his factory job an hour later, the house was full of loud singing coming from upstairs. There was an empty vanilla wafer box on the kitchen table.

"This little light of mine, I'm gonna let it shine!"

"Oh, man! Not the sister-thing again!" he yelled. But no one heard him over the laughter, which was even louder than the singing.

Another Home

That evening, after a quick dinner, Melody's mother drove the girls to choir rehearsal. Yvonne decided to tag along since their father was working a double shift and Dwayne was working an evening shift. Melody had been so busy getting her homework done that she hadn't had a chance to tell her mother about Val's move until they were all in the car.

"Mommy," Melody said from the backseat, "I got a letter from Val today. She said they're moving to Detroit, and they're coming as soon as school is over!"

Mommy looked at Melody in the rearview mirror. She didn't seem surprised.

"Yes, Big Momma told me a few weeks ago," Mommy said. "Until they find a house of their own, they'll be staying with Big Momma and Poppa."

Melody's grandparents lived just a few blocks away from the Ellisons. "That means I can walk over to see Val all the time," Melody announced. "We can do everything together!" *I couldn't have come up with a better plan myself,* she thought.

"Val has lived in Birmingham her whole life," Lila told Melody matter-of-factly. "Detroit sure is different. It's going to take her a while to get used to things."

Yvonne nodded. "I hope she'll like it here."

"Of course she will, Vonnie . . ." Melody said. But then she was quiet for a moment. Melody realized that she'd lived her whole life in the same house. It wouldn't be easy if she had to leave her neighborhood.

"Do you think Val is bringing her bike?" Lila asked, breaking the silence in the car.

"I don't know," Mommy answered. "All of their belongings will be coming on a moving truck later. The bike might take a while, so you girls will have to share some of your things with Val. You'll have to—"

"—make it work!" both Mommy and Melody said at the same time. Melody sounded exactly like Mommy, which made everyone laugh as they pulled up in front of New Hope Baptist Church.

When Melody got out of the car, she heard the
voices of the adult choir floating out of the open doors.
She ran up the steps into the church and sat on the first
pew inside the door. She closed her eyes and soaked in
the sounds.

"This is my story, this is my song." A single soprano
voice hit the notes and sang the words beautifully,
clearly. The music echoed inside Melody's body. She
opened her eyes and looked at the tall stained-glass
windows. On Sunday mornings, they sparkled like
jewels when the sunshine poured in.

Melody's sisters soon slid onto the bench, one
on either side, and she was squeezed between them
just like when she was small and Yvonne snuck her
lemon drops to keep her from wiggling during the
service. Melody smiled to herself at the memory. Now
that she was older, she didn't wiggle during church.
She listened to the pastor and to the music. She loved
the Sundays when the children's choir sang and she
stood in front, looking out at her family. Melody also
loved the Sundays when she sat in the pews with her
whole family. It was one of the few times they were all
together. *And soon Val will be here, too!* she thought.

Melody listened to the soloist sing the last lines of the hymn.

Watching and waiting, looking above,
Filled with His goodness, lost in His love.

That's how Melody felt in church. There was goodness all around. When the song ended, it seemed that her heart beat a little bit differently.

Melody was still swaying to the tune inside her head when Miss Dorothy walked past them, shuffling her sheet music.

"Hey, there's Miss Dorothy. Let's go." Lila pulled Melody up. The adults filed out of the choir stand, some going home after their long workday. Some, who were the parents of the children, went to sit in the back of the church to watch and wait.

Kids started filling in the choir stand. Melody saw Sharon run in, and she watched Diane take her seat in the front row.

As everyone gathered, Miss Dorothy started playing the piano softly. She knew everything about music. Like Big Momma, Miss Dorothy knew just how to talk to a singer to help make her voice better. And like Big Momma, Miss Dorothy could read and play from sheet music, or she could hear a tune and then play it herself without any music at all.

Melody thought Miss Dorothy was pretty amazing. She wished she could have heard her and Big Momma sing together back in the day. That would have been amazing, too.

When all the children were in place, Miss Dorothy walked in front of the choir and stood with her hands clasped behind her back. That was the sign for everyone to stop talking.

"All right, choir," she said. "On Sunday we'll be honoring all the New Hope mothers. We want to do our very best, don't we?"

"Yes, Miss Dorothy!"

"Remember that this will be our last choir rehearsal for this school year," Miss Dorothy went on. "I know all of you will spend some time singing over the summer. When school begins in September, we'll begin practicing for Youth Day. Melody, our soloist—I want you to find a song to sing. Your grandmother and I will start working on it with you over the summer if you'd like."

"Yes, Miss Dorothy," Melody said happily.

Diane leaned over to the girl next to her and loudly whispered, "If *I* were doing a solo, I wouldn't need the whole summer to practice."

Melody felt her face burn with hot embarrassment. Yvonne, who was sitting in the back of the church, stood up and crossed her arms over her chest. Melody was afraid she might say something, but then Miss Dorothy cleared her throat. Yvonne sat down again.

"Remember, even when one of us does a solo, we all work together," Miss Dorothy said sternly. "We all support one another. That's very important in a choir. The chorus helps the soloist. The soloist helps the chorus. Let's *all* remember that." She clicked her baton on the edge of the piano. "Now, choir, rise!"

Everyone stood. After Miss Dorothy led the group in vocal warm-ups, she repositioned the microphone in front of Diane, who was doing a solo for Mother's Day.

Diane stood straight and tall. She didn't blink. She didn't seem nervous at all. Melody had to admit that when she thought of her own faraway solo, she thought about what could go wrong. When Diane sang by herself, she acted as if she expected that everything would go right. She had what Dwayne called "stage presence."

Miss Dorothy stood at her piano and began playing. She played and directed and sang, all at the same time. Melody had always found it fascinating that she could do everything at once.

Diane sang the first line of the song. *"Be not dismayed whate'er betide . . ."*

The other children hummed in the background while Miss Dorothy played the chords. Diane sang the rest of the verse, and then the chorus came in with the refrain.

> *God will take care of you,*
> *Through every day, o'er all the way;*
> *He will take care of you,*
> *God will take care of you.*

Miss Dorothy stopped playing. "Sopranos, I can't really hear you. Let's try that again," she called out.

Melody looked at Yvonne, who was watching her. Yvonne cupped her hand behind her ear and grinned. She was telling Melody to sing out. When the choir began again, Melody heard Lila clearly in the row behind her, and Sharon beside her. Encouraged by their voices and by Yvonne's smile, Melody sang louder. Miss Dorothy nodded her approval.

"Well done," Miss Dorothy said. "Let's go on to 'His Eye Is on the Sparrow.'"

Miss Dorothy played the first chords. Diane began to sing again, and she did sound wonderful. Melody looked out and saw Mommy come in to sit down beside Yvonne. When it was time for the chorus, Melody sang out with all her heart.

> *I sing because I'm happy. I sing because I'm free.*
> *His eye is on the sparrow, and I know He watches me.*

Melody felt the entire choir's sound swell around her, and she was filled with a peaceful calm that made her feel happy and free.

After school the next day, Melody was sprawled on Big Momma's living room rug watching an old movie on TV. In it, a lady was coming home after a long trip and her friends gave her a "Welcome Back" party.

Melody sat up, hugging her knees. It would be a great idea to have a party for Val! They could have cookies and punch, and she could make a big sign that said "Welcome." She could pick some flowers from her garden—pink ones, because that was Val's favorite color.

Melody didn't have any homework to do, so she could start on the sign right away. She got up to get the art supplies Big Momma kept in a shoebox. Big Momma called it the "just in case" box, just in case somebody wanted to create something beautiful.

Melody found the box in the dining room and set it on the table. Then she headed back into the living room to get the construction paper from its spot in the piano bench. Big Momma came downstairs and shut off the TV.

"Big Momma, I think we should have a welcome party for Val and her parents," Melody said excitedly. "I'm going to make a banner with all their names on it."

Big Momma smiled in approval. "That sounds like a fine idea," she said. "You go on and work quietly in the kitchen, though. It's time for my first afternoon lesson."

Melody gathered her supplies and went to the kitchen, closing the door behind her as the doorbell rang. She arranged her crayons on the table, spread her paper just so, and carefully began to outline the word "WELCOME" in big block letters. She could hear the low hum of Big Momma's voice, a few piano chords, and then a familiar child's voice.

It was Diane Harris! Melody stopped working to listen.

The metronome that Big Momma used to show her students how fast or how slow to play their music started to *tick, tick, tick*! Diane's fingers fumbled over the piano keys. "Try again," Big Momma said calmly.

The choppy playing started and stopped, and then started over very slowly.

"Go on, go on." Big Momma sounded encouraging. But suddenly the piano was silent.

"Mrs. Porter, I can't do it!" Diane said. "I'll never play the piano as well as I can sing."

What had happened to Diane's bossy gym voice, Melody wondered. *And her sure and steady choir voice?* She sounded just the way Melody felt about doing a solo—nervous.

"Don't fret," Big Momma said to Diane. "This is new for you. Sometimes people are afraid of what they don't know."

Melody felt that Big Momma was speaking directly to her about the Youth Day solo.

Big Momma went on. "You have to take your time, and open your heart to learning. It may not be easy, but the things worth having usually don't come easily."

"Do you really think so?" Diane asked.

"I really do," Big Momma assured her. "You can shine with this instrument if you work hard enough."

In the kitchen, Melody smiled. *Maybe,* she thought, *Diane and I are more alike than we are different.* Melody picked up her crayon again, and drew a big yellow sun in the corner of her sign.

Dances and Dollars

*O*n Thursday afternoon, Poppa picked Melody up from school so that she could help him in his flower shop. Poppa knew all about growing things. Melody knew that back in Alabama he had grown vegetables and fruit trees as well as peanuts on his farm, and he had an enormous flower garden. He'd taught Melody how to plan a garden and how to care for it through all the different seasons. When her flowers bloomed, Melody loved to pick a bouquet and arrange it so that all the blossoms looked their best. Putting different colors and shapes together reminded her of different voices blending together in the choir. Melody had learned so much that now Poppa let her work in the shop sorting his weekly flower shipment and getting ready for the big weekend orders.

Melody settled back in the worn seat of his old work truck. It smelled like warm soil and flower petals. She inhaled deeply.

"How was school today?" Poppa asked, shifting gears.

Melody was distracted for a moment because she was watching people drive. Daddy said she was a true daughter of Detroit, the Motor City—the place where so many cars and trucks were built. Melody dreamed of driving her own car one day. She'd play the radio loud and sing along, maybe to one of Dwayne's hits . . .

"Melody?"

"Oh! Sorry, Poppa. School was okay."

"Just okay?" He gave her a curious look. "Hmm. Well, I have an idea that I think is more than okay."

Melody took her eyes off the sleek blue Thunderbird hardtop car passing by. "What is it?"

Poppa laughed. "*Now* I have your attention!" He slowed on 12th Street in front of his shop, Frank's Flowers, and pulled the truck around to the delivery entrance at the back. "How would you like to make a special arrangement for your mother and Big Momma for Mother's Day?"

"Yes!" Melody said, jumping out of the truck.

They stepped into the workroom, which was one of Melody's favorite places. The walls were lined with shelves that held vases of every shape and size, rolls of ribbon, and dozens of flowerpots and baskets. An old wooden worktable stretched along the length of the wall, and shears, floral tape, pins, and other supplies were arranged neatly on its surface. There was always music on the radio. This afternoon it was jazz. She recognized the saxophone sound because Daddy used to play one.

Melody dropped her book bag beside the door. There was a long cardboard box at one end of the table.

"Go on, look," Poppa said. Melody took a deep breath and carefully lifted the top off with both hands.

"Ohhh!" she gasped, smiling up at him. Inside the box wasn't candy, or toys, or anything else that would delight most nine-year-olds. The box was filled with flowers and feathery green ferns. "Red roses!" she said, taking a long sniff of their sweetness. Roses were Big Momma's favorite. "And yellow lilies, and pink freesia."

"Somebody knows her flowers," her grandfather said, taking a delicate china vase from the shelf.

Melody looked up at him proudly. "Can I really make this one all by myself?"

He tilted his head to one side, and the sun from the windows made his silver beard shine. "Yes you can, Little One," Poppa said. "When you're done, we'll leave it here in the cooler so it stays fresh. I'll bring it to the house early Sunday morning, and I'll hide it so your grandmother doesn't see it until after church. Watch out for the thorns."

"I will!" Melody said. She opened a drawer and took out the girl-size gardening gloves that she kept at the store. She pulled on the gloves, climbed up on a stool, and carefully picked up one of the roses. She was so busy imagining just how she would mix the colors and flowers in the vase that she didn't notice Poppa leaving the workroom.

Melody hummed along with the music as she clipped the ends of the stems carefully, the way Poppa had shown her, so the flowers could "drink" more water when she put them into the vase.

She ignored the tinkling of the bell on the front door as customers came and went. But when the telephone rang, she heard a voice that wasn't Poppa's say, "Hello. Frank's Flowers." It was Yvonne!

Melody put down her shears and peeked out front.

Poppa was talking to a customer in front of the huge cooler full of dozens of different types of flowers and greenery. Yvonne was standing behind the counter near the cash register. She was wearing her best pleated skirt and stockings, and her straightened hair was pulled back by a headband.

"What are you doing here?" Melody asked after Yvonne hung up the phone.

Yvonne didn't look happy. "I'm taking a break from my summer job hunt."

"Why?" Melody was trying to pay attention, but she noticed a pretty yellow flower in the cooler that she'd never seen before. It would be a perfect addition to her Mother's Day arrangement, she thought.

"I just applied for a job at the bank. The newspaper said they were hiring students for the summer, but no luck for me."

"Maybe the jobs are all full, and they don't need anybody else," Melody suggested.

"That's what the manager told me, but it wasn't true. He didn't even look at my application. A white girl about my age went into his office after me, and I heard him say they still had several summer positions open."

Melody jerked her head away from the cooler. "Is that the same bank where Mommy took me to open my savings account?"

Yvonne flushed angrily in answer. She looked as if she might cry.

Melody was outraged. "If they won't give my sister a job because she's black, then I'm going to take my money to a different bank."

Yvonne tried to smile. "Thanks, Dee-Dee."

"I'm serious," Melody said. The hurt on her sister's face made Melody think about something from a long time ago.

Once when Melody was only four and everyone else was already going to school, her grandparents had taken her south to see their cousins. It was very hot, and the lemonade in Big Momma's thermos was gone. Melody was still thirsty, so when Poppa stopped at a gas station in Alabama, Melody begged for a drink. There was a Coca-Cola machine, red and white and shiny. Poppa had given her a nickel so that she could buy an ice-cold soda pop. But when they got closer,

Big Momma said, "Stop, baby."

"I want a drink!" Little Melody had stomped her foot.

"I know," Big Momma said, "but we can't today. The machine is broken. Put your money in your pocket now."

Big Momma had taken Melody's hand to guide her away, and as Melody cried and followed, a little blonde girl about her size went to the machine. She stood on tiptoe and dropped a coin in. Then she reached in and pulled a frosty bottle out of the machine.

"It's not broken!" Melody had shouted. "It's not! I want a soda pop, too!" she'd cried, pulling against Big Momma's arm. Melody remembered crying for a long time, and none of Big Momma's other treats could make her feel better.

It wasn't until she was older and she could read that she understood. A few years later they were again driving south and stopped at a station, this time in Tennessee. Melody got out to stretch her legs, and she saw the same kind of soda machine. There was a sign above the machine that said "Whites Only." That's when Melody realized that the machine in

Alabama must have had the same kind of sign.

When they got back to Detroit, Melody had asked Big Momma why she hadn't told her about the sign the first time.

"Because it hurt me too much," Big Momma said. "I didn't want it to hurt you, too."

Melody's memory faded as the bell on the door of the flower shop tinkled, but her determination to go to the bank the first chance she had did not.

Two teenage boys had wandered into the store, and the girls turned their attention to them. They seemed lost. Poppa was still busy, so Yvonne greeted them.

"You sell corsages?" one of them asked sheepishly.

Melody smiled. She knew that a corsage was the tiny flower arrangement that girls wore to dances and proms.

Yvonne looked very businesslike. "Yes," she said. "Are you looking for a corsage to pin on her dress, or for her to wear on her wrist?"

"I dunno," the boy said.

"How much do they cost?" the other boy asked.

"How much do you have?" Yvonne asked.

"One dollar!" they both said at the same time.

Yvonne rolled her eyes, and Melody tried not to laugh. One dollar wasn't enough money to buy a very fancy corsage. But she could tell that Yvonne had a plan. Poppa, finished with his customer, was watching.

"Well," Yvonne said, "we can give you a special prom deal. Two single carnations with two ribbons for one dollar! We'll even match the color of the ribbons to the young lady's dress."

Melody saw Poppa's eyebrows rise.

"For real?" The first boy was shocked.

"Tell your friends," Yvonne said. "I know there are three dances at different high schools next week. This special runs only till Wednesday."

"Cool! We'll spread the word! Do we pay now?" the second boy asked.

"Yes." Yvonne picked up a receipt book from the counter. Melody went over to her grandfather.

"Poppa, I think you should give Yvonne a job."

"I'm thinking the same thing, Little One," he said.

"Mommy!" Melody yelled, as soon as she and Yvonne got home. "Mommy!"

The radio was playing a Smokey Robinson song when Melody burst into the kitchen. Her mother was snapping her fingers to the beat while she danced in front of the refrigerator. There was a stack of her students' math papers on the kitchen table and a pot of spaghetti sauce bubbling on the stove.

Mommy enjoyed music by dancing to it. Any other time Melody would have joined her, but not today.

"What in the world is it?" Mommy asked, putting a lid on the pot. She stopped dancing and turned down the sound on the radio.

"Yvonne didn't get a job, so I have to go to the bank!" Melody plopped into a chair.

"Explain," Mommy said, glancing at Yvonne. Yvonne only shrugged and tilted her head toward Melody.

"Yvonne tried to get a job at the bank, but they wouldn't hire her because she's black." Melody was angry again just thinking about the whole thing. "I want to protest by taking my money out. Will you take me to the bank tomorrow?"

"Yes," Mommy said, without asking any other questions.

♫

The very next day after school, Melody held her
mother's hand as they walked through the lobby of
Detroit Bank. Melody had worn her best school jumper,
and she carried her bank-account book. Melody looked
around the large room. She and her mother were the
only black people in sight, and she was the only child.

Melody and her mother stood in a short line, and
for a few seconds Melody felt uncomfortable. Was
everyone looking at her? Her cheeks were suddenly
very warm, and her fingers felt sweaty as she curled
them around her bankbook. *Can I do this?* Melody
wondered. She had asked her mother in the car just
what to say and how to say it, but now Melody was
nervous. Then she saw a girl Yvonne's age working
behind a desk. She was white. Did she get a job when
Yvonne couldn't even apply? Melody took a deep
breath and reminded herself that she was standing up
for her sister—and for making things fair.

When it was her turn, Melody let go of Mommy's
hand and stepped up to the counter, which came up to
her shoulders. Melody made herself as tall as she could.

The bank teller was an older white woman with red hair. "I would like to withdraw my money," Melody told her.

"And how much would you like to withdraw?"

"All of it."

The teller raised her eyebrows. "Are you sure?" she asked kindly.

"Yes," Melody said firmly. "My sister is really good with money and numbers, but this bank wouldn't let her apply for a summer job because she's black. That's not fair."

The teller looked confused for a moment. "Do you understand, dear, that if you withdraw everything you'll close your account?" She glanced over Melody's head in Mommy's direction.

Melody slid her bankbook across the counter. Her insides were quivering a little, but she looked straight at the teller. "Yes. I understand. This bank discriminates against black people. I don't want to keep my money here anymore."

It seemed like forever before the woman finally nodded and picked up Melody's bankbook. Melody watched the teller count out ten one-dollar bills and put them into a small envelope. Melody noticed that the girl behind the desk was staring with her mouth open, as if she didn't believe a kid could do something this important. Melody turned away.

Her mother smiled and took her hand. "Good job," she said. "You know, your daddy says voting is a way to speak up for what we believe. Money has a voice, too. What we do with it says a lot about what we believe."

Melody blew out a breath of relief. "Thanks, Mommy."

"I'm proud of you, Melody," her mother said as they walked out side by side.

Mother's Day Surprises

♪ CHAPTER 6 ♪

*m*elody woke up early on Mother's Day. She rolled over and nudged Lila. "Get up! We've got to make breakfast for Mommy before church," she said. Lila groaned and rolled back over.

"Hurry," Melody told her. Melody expected to have to wake Yvonne, too. But when Melody looked over at her other sister's bed, it was empty. Yvonne was already up.

Melody hopped out of bed and ran across the hall to the bathroom. "Vonnie! Vonnie, we have to get breakfast," she whispered so as not to wake their mother.

Her sister nudged the bathroom door open with her foot as she finished tying a scarf over her head.

Melody raised an eyebrow. "Don't you usually take

that *off* in the morning?" Yvonne often wore the scarf to keep her hair from getting too tangled up while she slept.

Yvonne only nodded. "Let's get the Mother's Day surprises started," she whispered, waving Melody down the stairs.

In the kitchen, Melody opened the fridge and took out orange juice and eggs. Yvonne made coffee. Lila finally came down, dragging Dwayne by the arm.

"So early," he said sleepily. "Why can't Mom just have toast and orange juice?"

"Because," Melody said, "today's a special day to celebrate her. I'm going out to pick some flowers. Why don't you set up the tray?"

He groaned just as Lila had.

Melody stepped out the back door and went to the garden she had planted along the side of the driveway. Only a few flowers had bloomed so early in the season. She picked what was most beautiful and took the bunch back inside to arrange it in a teacup.

Dwayne had the tray ready. He had laid a fresh cloth towel over it, then a plate that matched the teacup, a paper napkin, and a fork. Melody placed the teacup of bright daffodils beside the plate, and then poured a glass of juice.

"Where's the coffee?" Melody asked.

"Coming," Lila answered.

Yvonne had already scrambled the eggs and made toast.

"She needs jam," Melody said.

"I'll get it." Lila went to the pantry and got an unopened jar of plum preserves that Big Momma had made last summer. "Are we ready?"

"Hey, did anybody remember to get a card?" Yvonne asked.

"I made one," Melody said. She ran to get it from its hiding place in the pantry, next to the box of Cheerios.

"Okay, everything is ready," Dwayne said. He picked up the tray, carefully carrying it up the stairs with his sisters following behind. At their parents' door, Melody raised her hand to knock.

"Hold it," Dwayne whispered.

"What?" Lila frowned.

"Let's not do the same old thing. Let's sing," Dwayne said.

"Ohhh! I like that!" Melody said. Dwayne bounced

his head as if he was listening to a beat. He quietly hummed a few notes. The girls hummed back. From inside their parents' room they heard Bo join in with a howl.

Dwayne laughed. "Of course we have the only dog in Detroit with perfect pitch," he said.

Melody knocked sharply on the door.

"Who is it?" Daddy said in his joking voice.

"It's me—I mean, it's us," Melody answered. "We're here with Mother's Day breakfast for Mommy."

"Come on," Daddy said.

Melody opened the door and they sang "*Happy Mother's Da-a-ay . . .*" together to Dwayne's new tune.

"That is wonderful!" Their mother clapped as Dwayne put the tray across her knees. "Thank you all." She eagerly looked at her breakfast. "Will!" she said. "They found plum preserves. I didn't know we had any left."

"Hey! I was hiding that for myself," Daddy said.

"I'll share," Mommy said. She broke off a corner of toast to feed to Bo.

While their mother ate, Melody, Dwayne, and Lila crowded onto the foot of the bed. "This certainly is an improvement over last year's Mother's Day breakfast," Daddy said, sneaking a bite of scrambled egg. "You delivered burnt pancakes."

Lila giggled. "That was Dwayne's fault."

"Oh, no it was *not*," Dwayne said. "That was Yvonne."

"Where *is* Yvonne?" Mommy asked.

Before anyone could answer, they heard water running in the bathroom. Melody looked at the clock on her parents' bedside table. "Lila! We have to get ready, too," she said, jumping off the bed. "Miss Dorothy asked us to be there early, so we can get one more practice in!"

An hour later, everyone was ready for church. Everyone except Yvonne. Melody tapped her foot and looked up the stairs anxiously, afraid they would be late. Both she and Lila had on the white blouses and navy blue skirts that the girls in the children's choir wore whenever they performed.

Dwayne came down wearing his dark suit and tie. Daddy called up the stairs. "Yvonne, this is not a beauty contest. This is church. We must go, or your sisters are going to be late."

"I'm coming!" Yvonne's voice floated downstairs.

Melody glanced at the living room clock and looked up the stairs again.

"Hurry up, Yvonne!" Melody said.

"On my way!"

Then came the biggest Mother's Day surprise. Yvonne walked slowly down the stairs. She wore a bright orange dress and heels. But as her entire body came into view, she was also wearing an Afro hairstyle. Her chin-length hair, which she usually straightened, was now a curly, crinkly globe standing out a few inches around her face.

Mommy gasped.

Dwayne chuckled.

"What did you do to your head?" Daddy asked in disbelief.

Melody looked at her mother and realized that for the first time ever, Mommy was speechless. No one they knew had ever worn an Afro. Melody and Lila and all their friends usually wore pigtails or braids so that their hair stayed neat, even when they ran around and played. Grown ladies like Mommy—and the Motown girl groups Melody admired—wore straightened hairstyles that were smooth and glossy and tidy. On special occasions, Melody got to wear her hair straightened, too.

"I'm going natural," Yvonne announced. "I'm honoring my African heritage. Happy Mother's Day, Mom. Do you like it?"

Mommy stared at Yvonne for a minute. "I—I don't really know how I feel yet," she said.

"I feel weird," Lila said.

Melody reached up to touch her sister's hair. It was tightly curled, soft, and springy. "It's nice," Melody said. "It's like a crown."

When they got into the station wagon, Dwayne complained that Yvonne's hair took up too much room. Daddy made him sit in the fold-down seat at the back.

As the Ellisons filed out of the car in front of the church, Melody heard whispers from the prim and proper ladies with straightened hair and fancy hats. "What sort of a hairdo is that?" one of them whispered to the others, not at all quietly. Melody knew that Yvonne heard them, too, but she just smiled. *She stands up for what she believes in*, Melody thought. *I'm so proud she's my big sister.*

The service was long, but Melody didn't mind. Pastor Daniels talked about how all people deserved respect, and how justice and fairness were ways of showing respect. Melody thought about her trip to the bank. Then the pastor talked about how important it was to respect, love, and obey your mother.

After he finished, Miss Dorothy went to the piano and raised both her hands. The children's choir stood up. As the music started, Melody looked out into the congregation and saw her mother in her usual seat right next to Big Momma. Both their hats were nodding in the air in time to the music. As Diane sang her solo, Melody kept her eyes on her mother and grandmother. When it was time for her to join in, she sang with love in every single note.

When the song ended, the congregation clapped and cheered. Pastor Daniels gave a single red or white rose to each of the mothers. Melody and Yvonne had tied ribbons to each flower at Poppa's shop yesterday.

As everyone sang the final song of the service together, Melody noticed three people coming into the church. *Who would show up now?* Melody wondered. Then her eyes grew wide. It was Charles and Tish and Val! Melody hadn't seen her cousin since last summer, but she knew it was her.

Val was wearing a frilly pink dress and pink socks with ruffles at the edges, and her hair was in a poufy ponytail tied up in a white bow. There was Cousin Charles, tall and skinny, with a mustache and a beard like Poppa, and Cousin Tish, as tall as Charles. She wore a hat with a huge feather that made her seem even taller.

Val looked at Melody and waved. Melody grinned. As soon as the song was over and Miss Dorothy gave the children permission to go, Melody pulled Sharon from her seat.

"My cousin's here. You have to meet her!" Melody said breathlessly. The two sped down the side aisle and zigzagged around chatting grown-ups to get to the back.

"Val!" Melody squealed, crushing Val's Sunday dress as she gave her an enormous hug.

"Dee-Dee!" Val knocked Melody off balance as she hugged back.

"You said you were coming when school was out," Melody said.

"I thought we were. But Mama and Daddy decided to start packing right after I wrote to tell you we were moving," Val explained. "We left yesterday. Daddy drove all night so that we could get here in time for church." Then she laughed. "I guess we didn't make it."

Melody linked arms with her cousin. "This is my best friend in Detroit, Sharon."

Sharon gave Val a shy smile. "Hi," she said.

"And Sharon, this is Val, my best friend from Alabama, and my best cousin, too."

Val stuck out a white-gloved hand to shake, and when Sharon grabbed it, the glove slipped off. The girls burst into giggles.

"Melody, I've gotta go—we're taking my grandma out to dinner. See you tomorrow! Remember, Matching Monday is blue!" Sharon vanished among the suits and dresses.

"What's Matching Monday?" Val asked. She took off her other glove and stuffed both of them into her little pink purse.

"Sharon and I wear the same color hair ribbons to

school on Mondays. When we were in kindergarten, we pretended that we were twins," Melody explained.

"That's funny! You don't look anything alike!"

"It's our little joke." Melody smiled. "Hey—I've got an idea. You can be part of Matching Mondays, too."

After hellos and hugs outside the church, everyone headed for their cars to ride to Big Momma and Poppa's house.

Melody didn't want Val out of her sight for even a moment. "Daddy," she called out, "can Val and I ride back with Poppa?" Her father nodded.

"What a great surprise," Melody said, giving Val's hand a squeeze. "I'm so glad you're here!"

A Family Reunion

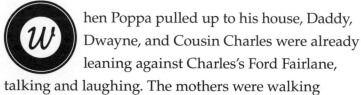hen Poppa pulled up to his house, Daddy, Dwayne, and Cousin Charles were already leaning against Charles's Ford Fairlane, talking and laughing. The mothers were walking slowly up the driveway, talking and laughing. Melody knew that the day was going to be full of talking and laughing.

"Look at you, man!" Charles thumped Dwayne on the back. "You weren't this tall last summer! Are you still singing?"

Melody saw Dwayne duck his head, but he answered, "Yeah, yeah I am."

"He's just playing with that music business in his spare time," Daddy said. "He's going to college in September."

Dwayne opened his mouth to say something, but

then closed it again. When Melody sighed, Val looked at her curiously. "What's that about?" she whispered.

Melody shook her head. "Tell you later. Look! Your mother and Big Momma have Yvonne cornered!"

Big Momma and Cousin Tish were standing on either side of Yvonne on the porch steps, studying her Afro while Mommy looked on.

"Oh!" Val whispered. "I wonder what Mama is saying." Cousin Tish had owned a hair salon in Birmingham. Melody loved the fact that she never knew what Tish's hair would look like when she saw her next. Each time it was a different style and color: curly and red, long and brown, short and black, or piled high and wavy like today. What would she think of Yvonne's crinkly crown?

"Let's hurry up so we can hear!" Melody said.

"Now, how did you get it to stand up?" Big Momma was asking.

"I have a special comb," Yvonne said.

"Some people don't like natural hair because it looks so different from what we're used to," Tish said. She looked at Yvonne thoughtfully. "I think that style suits your face. I'm going to open a salon here as soon as I find a spot. I wonder if my future Detroit clients would like a style like that?"

"I'm not sure how many young women are as radical as our Yvonne," Mommy said, opening the front door.

"What does 'radical' mean?" Melody asked.

"It means somebody who's willing to raise her voice," Yvonne said.

"Willing to raise her hair, too!" Mommy said as she went inside.

Melody and Val followed, but they all bumped into a traffic jam just inside the living room. Everyone was looking up at the arch where Poppa had quickly hung Melody's colorful construction-paper signs all the way across, saying "Welcome Charles, Tish, and Val." Underneath, on a small round table, was the Mother's Day flower arrangement Melody had made at Poppa's shop.

"Oh!" Tish clapped. "Who made all this loveliness?"

"Melody did," Lila said, peering around for her sister.

"Melody?" Mommy called, and Melody made her way to the dining room with Val right behind.

"Thank you, honey!" Tish gave her a hug. "There's nothing like being around family."

"And there's nothing like Big Momma's fried chicken," Charles said, as Yvonne and Mommy brought plates and bowls of food from the kitchen.

"Come on, everyone," Big Momma called. "Let's eat."

There was so much talking and laughing that dinner went on and on. Everyone was so busy catching up on cousins and old friends that Big Momma served a second round of cake and ice cream.

"Say, Frances!" Charles said, scraping the last of the crumbs off his plate. "This reminds me of the first time you made a triple-chocolate cake. It was kind of lopsided, remember?"

"Lopsided?" Dwayne laughed. "Are you kidding?"

"No, he's not kidding," Mommy said. "And yes, I remember. I was a new wife, and I didn't bake very well."

"What your mother did was nothing to laugh at," Daddy said. "I had dreamed about chocolate when I was overseas during the war. I saw a cake like that in the window of a bakery in town the day I got back."

"Why didn't you just go into the bakery and buy it?" Melody asked.

Mommy poured more coffee for the grown-ups. "I tried," she said. "That bakery refused to serve Negroes. I was so angry that I decided to try to make the cake myself."

Daddy said, "There we were, fighting for freedom for the world, and we didn't have it when we got back home."

"But you two were Tuskegee Airmen!" Dwayne said. "I mean, you got a medal, Dad!"

"Yes. I was the most highly trained mechanic in my unit. I kept those planes in top flying condition. But when I left the service, I couldn't get a job in my home-town. I had to move all the way to Detroit, and even up here I had to start at the bottom doing the most back-breaking jobs at the auto factory."

Charles sighed. "Things sure haven't changed much. Here I am, moving to Detroit for the same reason."

"What do you mean?" Daddy asked.

"The black hospital where I worked closed down," Charles explained. "I tried to get a job at one of the white hospitals, but no one would hire me. I'm a licensed pharmacist, but it seemed as if people only saw me as some black man they couldn't be bothered with."

Melody thought about what had happened to Yvonne at the bank. "That's wrong," she whispered to her sister. Yvonne looked at Melody and nodded. So did Mommy.

Charles's face was serious. "I got stopped by a cop when I was on my way to a job interview. I was wearing a suit and tie, not doing anything wrong, but the police still treated me like a criminal. When the hospital closed, I just felt it was time for us to get out of Birmingham."

"But if everybody like you and Tish leaves, who's going to stay and fight?" Yvonne asked.

"Girl, if you miss a day of work to participate in a march or a protest, you can lose your job," Charles said. "I have a family to support. I couldn't risk it."

"But things are changing," Yvonne insisted.

"Yes, but things are also getting tense," Charles said. He put his coffee cup down. "It was bad enough when white people threw food at peaceful protesters or pulled them off their seats at a lunch counter. But now the police are setting dogs and fire hoses on people!"

Tish tapped her bright red fingernails on the table. "Charles and I have been talking about this for months. There's a lot of good happening in the South, but some of it is getting dangerous. The police turned those hoses on children. *Children!*"

Melody knew what Tish was talking about. Everyone did. It had happened last week, and news of it was still on the TV every night. Melody had seen black schoolkids in Birmingham, singing and carrying signs. Then policemen chased them, and turned giant hoses on them. The blasts of water were so strong that they knocked the children to the ground.

Melody glanced at Val. Val looked down at her dish of ice cream.

"Those police in Birmingham were wrong," Big Momma said. She reached over and gently raised Val's chin with her hand. "And those children were very brave."

"I don't see why we have to fight fire with fire, as the old saying goes," Mommy said. "Dr. King speaks against hatred and fear. He believes we can change hearts and laws without violence."

"He's coming to Detroit next month," Poppa said, "making a speech down at Cobo Hall."

Melody felt as if something big was happening right here at her grandparents' table. She wasn't quite sure what it was, but she had a feeling that some kind of change was in the air.

"I heard people at the flower shop talking about it," Yvonne said. "There's going to be a march. It's called the Walk to Freedom!"

"Yes, our union is marching," Daddy said. Melody saw her mother give her father an approving look. "We don't have the same sort of segregation as in the South," Daddy continued, "but we need more good jobs for black people here in Detroit."

"And better, less crowded schools for black children," Mommy added. "And fair housing laws."

"You make it sound like Detroit is a mess," Dwayne piped up. "Black people like Poppa have businesses—and Tish, you want to open a business, right? Well, you can! And don't forget that this is where the music starts. Hitsville, U.S.A. Motown." Dwayne started snapping his fingers and humming a tune. Everyone around the table started laughing.

Daddy rolled his eyes at Dwayne, but he was smiling when he said, "I think we should all take part in the march as a family."

"Go, Daddy!" Yvonne clapped her hands.

"I don't know, Cousin," Charles said. "We're staying out of this marching business. I just want to get my family settled in, find a place to live. We're looking to get a fresh start here in Detroit."

There was silence for a moment. "I understand how you must feel," Mommy said gently, looking at Charles. Then she turned to Daddy. "I would like to hear what Dr. King has to say in person."

"That young man is a powerful preacher," Poppa said. "I'd like to hear him too."

Big Momma motioned to Lila. "Put the date on my kitchen calendar, Lila. When is it, Will?"

"June twenty-third," Daddy said. "Whoever's going will meet right here, so we can walk to freedom together."

After dinner, Melody and Val sat side by side on

♪ A Family Reunion ♪

Big Momma's sofa. "Are you tired after the long car ride from Birmingham?" Melody asked as Dwayne played his still-wordless tune. When Val didn't answer, Melody tilted her head sideways to look at her cousin. "What's wrong?"

Val shrugged, so Melody dragged her up and pulled her past Dwayne at the piano and out the front door. She sat down on the top step. Val hesitated a moment, then smoothed the skirt of her dress and sat down too.

"I'm happy to see you, and everybody," Val said quietly. "But everything happened so fast with our move. I couldn't really say good bye to my friends the way I wanted to." She sighed. "I just don't feel like I have any kind of home anymore. You wouldn't understand."

"Tell me what you mean," Melody said. She *wanted* to understand.

"Detroit isn't home," Val said. "Home's not home anymore either. I used to feel safe in Birmingham. Now there's always police, and people in the streets getting arrested. I knew one of those kids who got knocked down by the water hose. She said it was really scary."

"Wow," Melody said. She told Val what Pastor Daniels had said that morning about everybody deserving justice. "Those kids stood up for themselves. That's really brave."

"I know," Val said, looking at their reflections in the toes of her patent leather shoes. "But we're just kids."

"But we still count," Melody said. "This is our world, too!" She told Val what she'd done at the bank when her sister couldn't get a job there.

"That's brave, too," Val said. She looked at Melody and smiled slowly. "I think living in Detroit is going to be *real* interesting."

"It will be, I promise!" Melody said.

"I want to help Val feel at home in Detroit," Melody said the very next afternoon as she and Lila walked home from school. "Let's take her to the library today."

"Sure, that sounds like fun," said Lila. "Val might like the craft class, too."

Melody smiled. Lila loved to make things as much as she loved to read. At first, she made toys from branches or scraps of wood. Then she started taking apart things around the house and trying to put them back together, like Dwayne's old record player. Now she was obsessed with the library's craft class.

The girls went home to drop off their book bags, change out of their school clothes, and have a snack. Lila also had to get the stack of library books she was returning. She had so many that Melody offered to help her carry them.

"Was this one any good?" Melody asked, holding up *The Kid's Book of Engineering*.

"Yes, it was," Lila said. "And that reminds me. Guess what happened this morning."

"What?"

"My teacher said she's nominated me for a science scholarship to a private high school."

"Wow!" Melody stopped and stared at her sister. "Wait till Mommy and Daddy find out!" Mommy always said that all of the Ellison kids were smart, but Melody thought Lila might be the smartest. She was good at math and science and reading. In fact, she was good in every subject.

"I don't know . . . it costs a lot of money," Lila muttered.

"Doesn't a scholarship mean you can go for free?" Melody asked, beginning to walk again.

"Maybe. The scholarship might not cover all the costs," Lila said. "And first I have to take a hard entrance exam to qualify for one."

"You can pass any test! You're a straight A student," Melody said. "Why are you worried?"

Lila looked at her. "For the same reason that you're worried about doing a solo for Youth Day even though you're a great singer."

Melody hadn't thought of it that way.

Big Momma was just finishing a music lesson with a student when Melody and Lila arrived. Val had been sitting at the kitchen table by herself, and she jumped up when Melody told her they were going to the library.

Big Momma smiled. "That's a good idea. You can get to know the neighborhood, Valerie. You girls go on, and be careful." Big Momma waved.

"Bye, Big Momma!" they sang together.

"Where is the library?" Val asked as they skipped down the porch steps.

"Not far," Melody told her. "Only nine blocks."

Val looked shocked. "My mama and daddy didn't let me walk that far by myself in Birmingham. Not with everything that was going on."

Melody nodded silently, thinking about yesterday's conversation. "Well, it won't take long to get to Duffield library," she said. "When school's out, Lila and I go a couple of times a week. We're both in the summer reading club. There are prizes and everything. There's lots of other stuff to do, too. There's a craft class, and a board-game club."

"So this is what you do all summer, when you're up here and not visiting us?" Val asked.

"Not *all* summer," Melody said. "We go swimming at the YWCA, and on weekends Mommy takes us across to Canada, and—"

"Canada?" Val repeated doubtfully.

"Yep. Canada is right across the river. We drive over the bridge and get there in no time at all," Lila said.

"There's so much stuff I don't know about this place." Val sounded interested.

"You can come with me to help Poppa at his flower shop," Melody suggested. "Or you can come and help me in my own garden," she added. "I could help you plant a garden at your new house, if you want."

"Yes, I'd like that a lot," Val told her. "I think Mama would, too. We could plant loads and loads of pink flowers! What else?"

Melody wrinkled her nose as she thought. Of course there would be barbecues and maybe a baseball game or two—

"I can think of something," Lila said mysteriously. "And it's coming up."

"What?" Val asked, confused.

Melody knew what Lila was talking about. "Look across the street," she said as they turned onto busy Grand Boulevard. Melody pointed to a two-story house with a big white sign across the front windows.

"Hitsville U.S.A.," Val read aloud. "Oh my gosh! Is that what Dwayne was talking about yesterday? That's Motown?"

"Yes!" Melody and Lila said together.

Val's eyes became so wide that she almost looked like a cartoon character. Lila burst out laughing.

"This is their recording studio," Melody said. She thought of Dwayne's big secret—the audition he was waiting for. But she didn't say anything.

"Have you ever seen anybody famous?" Val seemed rooted to the sidewalk, but there wasn't anybody around.

"Well, not yet," Melody admitted.

"Come on," Lila waved them along. "Enough star-watching for today. Maybe we can catch sight of The Marvelettes over the summer!"

"The Marvelettes!" Melody and Val sighed together. Melody started humming the tune to their song "Please Mr. Postman," and Lila and Val hummed along.

Four blocks farther down they came to the large, low limestone building that was the Duffield branch of the Detroit Public Library. At the steps, Val stopped to stare. "The colored library is really big!" she exclaimed.

"Colored library?" Lila asked.

Val looked confused. "Isn't this where we're going? The colored library?"

"It's just a library," Melody said. "Anybody can go to any public library."

"You're in Detroit now," Lila reminded Val. "Not Birmingham."

"And we go in the front doors, just like this?" Val was wide-eyed again.

"That's right." Melody shifted her pile of books and skipped up the steps. "Have you ever read *The Secret Garden*?" she asked Val. "These kids find a hidden gate, and all kinds of stuff happens. It's one of my all-time favorite books."

Val shook her head. "I haven't read it, but I bet I'll like it."

"How do you know?" Lila asked.

"I'll like it because Dee-Dee likes it," Val said. "That's how friends are."

"Come on, cousin-friend," Melody said, opening the door. "I'll show you the children's section!"

Signs and Songs

♪ CHAPTER 8 ♪

I t was finally June, and school was finally over. Melody had thought it would never end! She burst through the front door of her house on the last day and tossed her book bag into a corner.

"I'm done, I'm done!" She did a little dance right on the living room rug while Lila came in behind her.

"Don't forget to pick that up," Lila told her, before tromping up the stairs with her book bag thumping.

"I guess you're glad school is out," Yvonne said from the dining room.

Melody nodded. "Yes, but Sharon's going to New Orleans tomorrow for the whole summer. I'm glad Val's here already. I can't wait to call her!"

"You don't have to wait," Val said as she appeared from the kitchen.

"You're here!" Melody laughed, rushing over to give her cousin a hug. "It has been so hard to sit in school knowing that you're done already."

"It's been just as hard waiting for y'all to finish!" Val said, sitting down at the dining room table. "Daddy's started his new job, and Mama's looking for a place for her salon, so I could use some company."

"Yvonne, how come you're not at the flower shop?" Melody asked.

"Poppa gave me the afternoon off to work on a special project," Yvonne said.

Melody noticed that the table was covered with poster boards, paints, crayons, and glue. "What are you making?"

"Signs for the Walk to Freedom," Val said proudly. "Look at the one I just painted."

Melody read the big blue words out loud. *Freedom Forever.* There were other slogans, too. *Justice for All! Fair Housing Now! Separate Is Not Equal!* "Wow. This is really cool," Melody said.

Yvonne nodded. "We're making as many as we can. I'll take them to the church. Someone there will pass them out on the Sunday of the march."

Lila came back down. She had changed out of her school clothes. "Oh, can I help?" she asked.

"Me, too?" Melody asked.

"Sure," Yvonne nodded. "But Melody, you'd better change out of your school clothes."

Melody hurried upstairs to put on a pair of shorts. When she came back, Dwayne was stomping through the back door, singing "Summertime." He stuck his head into the dining room.

Melody was surprised to see him. He was usually still at the factory at this time of day. She looked at the clock and then at Dwayne. When she opened her mouth to say something, Dwayne pulled his finger and thumb across his lips. *This has something to do with his secret,* Melody thought. She didn't say a word.

"What's up with all this?" Dwayne asked.

"Don't get too close," Yvonne warned. "You'll mess up our posters."

"They're for the freedom walk," Melody told him.

"I am not going on any freedom walk," he said. "I've got better things to do."

"Like what?" Lila asked suspiciously.

"Like none of your business," Dwayne answered.

"What could be more important than freedom?" Yvonne asked.

"Being lead singer of Dwayne and The Detroiters," he said.

Yvonne looked annoyed.

Lila said, "You'd better be thinking about college, too. You know what Daddy says."

"Plenty of people do just fine without a college degree!" he said. "Look at Tish!" He went into the kitchen.

Val stopped tracing the word "Justice" and pointed her pencil at Lila. "My mama says it's just as important for a colored person to run a business as it is to go to college."

Yvonne smiled. "That's because Tish is a successful business owner."

"Like Poppa, and the people who run the bakery," Melody added.

"And Berry Gordy at Motown. He's running a successful music business!" Dwayne called from the kitchen. A few minutes later, he came back into the dining room holding a saucer stacked with two peanut butter and jelly sandwiches. "Music is a *business*!"

"Bet you won't tell Daddy that," Lila said.

Dwayne rolled his eyes in her direction, and then nodded at Melody as he stood in the middle of the floor eating. "So how's *your* music coming?" he asked.

"My song?" Melody hadn't stopped thinking about her Youth Day solo. There were so many she liked. "I haven't picked one yet," she confessed.

Dwayne shoved the last corner of one of the sandwiches into his mouth and pulled Melody away from the table. "You love singing, don't you?"

"Yes," she said.

"And you want to do this solo, don't you?"

"Yes!" Melody answered right away.

"Here's the thing about that, Dee-Dee." Dwayne sat on the sofa so that he and Melody were eye to eye. He looked and sounded serious when he talked about music with Melody. "The songs you sing don't just have to be right for your voice, or for whatever audience you're singing for, okay? Your song has to *feel* right. The words have to mean something special to you. When they do, amazing things happen."

"Is that why all your songs are so good?" Melody asked.

Dwayne nodded. "I kind of think so."

Melody wondered if this was why Diane always sounded so good, too. Did the songs she sang *feel* right to her? Suddenly the tunes from dozens of songs popped into Melody's head: songs that made her happy, silly nursery rhymes that made her laugh, church songs, dancing songs, sad songs.

"Oh, I can see your music brain working hard!" Dwayne said, and Melody realized that her shoulders were moving to the music in her head. She stopped and laughed.

"See what I mean?" Dwayne smiled at her.

"Yes," Melody said. "But how will I know which one is right?"

"You'll know." Dwayne patted her shoulder. "You'll know when—"

Dwayne stopped talking when he heard their mother's key turn in the front door.

"Dwayne! Get off the sofa!" Melody whispered. "You're still in your work clothes."

He jumped and ran.

"I'm home!" Mommy called out the way she always did when she came in. "And I've brought company!"

"Hi, Mommy!" Melody rushed to give her mother a hug. She looked curiously at the older woman who followed Mommy in. Her hair was snow white and she carried a wooden cane, but her dark face had no wrinkles at all. The woman's sharp dark eyes twinkled as she looked back at Melody.

"This is Miss Esther Collins. She's just joined our church, and she's helping me on the finance committee. Miss Esther, this is my youngest, Melody. And those are my other two daughters, Yvonne and Lila, and Cousin Valerie."

"Hello, Miss Esther!" the girls said.

"Hello there," Miss Esther said in a high, quivery voice.

"Please sit down while I get those phone numbers for you," Mommy said, going upstairs.

Instead of sitting, Miss Esther headed to the dining room, clicking her cane across the floor. "You young people are always busy," she said. "What's this you're doing?"

"We're making posters for the Walk to Freedom," Melody told her.

"Oh, yes." Miss Esther nodded. "It's going to be

quite an event. That young Dr. King is speaking."

Yvonne looked up, impressed. "You know about it?"

Miss Esther nodded. "We've been fighting this fight for a long time, child. You're never too old or too young to stand up for justice."

Just then Mommy returned, carrying a sheet of yellow paper. At the same moment, the sound of a new Miracles hit came from the kitchen.

"What's that record?" Miss Esther asked. "Is that one of those Motown boys?"

"It's not a record," Melody said. "That's our brother, Dwayne!"

Miss Esther looked surprised. "My! He could be a professional singer."

Melody looked proud. "He sure could."

"After college," Mommy said gently, handing the yellow sheet of phone numbers to Miss Esther.

Miss Esther looked thoughtful. "Nothing takes the place of a good education," she said. "But each of us has our own path to follow."

It almost sounded to Melody as if Miss Esther knew Dwayne's secret.

"Let me walk you out," Mommy said brightly.

"Good-bye, all!" Miss Esther waved. "You take care of this wonderful family, Frances," she said.

When Mommy and Miss Esther stepped out of the house, Melody threw open the kitchen door. "Hey, Dwayne," she said. "Guess what?"

"What?" Dwayne popped his head out.

"Somebody just thought you were a record!"

"No joke?" He chuckled and walked through the dining room with his head held high in the air. "See?" he said to Yvonne over his shoulder as he passed. "I'm not walking to freedom. I'm *singing* my way up."

The Power Inside

A week later, Melody and Lila were in the kitchen eating bologna and cheese sandwiches and drinking ginger ale when they heard someone at the front door.

Lila stopped chewing. "Who in the world is that in the middle of the day?"

Melody put her cup down. "Maybe Yvonne came home early."

Before Lila could call out, the first notes of one of Dwayne's tunes came from their living room. Three male voices harmonized to the music.

"It's Dwayne and his group!" Lila whispered.

"Where's the music coming from? We don't have a piano," Melody whispered back.

Lila rolled her eyes. "Obviously they got a tape recorder from somewhere!" She got up and motioned for Melody to follow. The two stood at the kitchen door, listening.

The song was so lively that Melody started dancing to the beat. Then she bumped the butter knife that Lila had left on the counter, and it clattered to the floor. The music stopped.

"Oops!" Lila snickered.

In a second, Dwayne swung the kitchen door open. "Are you two snooping?"

"Sort of," Melody said.

Instead of getting upset, Dwayne shrugged. "So why don't you come on in? Be our audience."

Lila headed for the living room, but Melody held back and grabbed her brother's arm. "Shouldn't you be at work?" she asked. Melody was still keeping Dwayne's secret about the Motown audition. Now it seemed as if Dwayne was keeping a secret from her.

"I'll tell you later," he whispered. "I promise."

Melody followed him to the living room and plopped onto the couch beside Lila, who was talking to Artie and Phil. Dwayne, Artie, and Phil had been friends forever. Melody's earliest memories were of the boys showing her how to beat the bottom of a saucepan with a wooden spoon like a drum, to keep up with their doo-wop beat. Big Momma had taught Dwayne piano, and he started making up his own music. For the last year, the three boys had been singing all over the city.

Dwayne seemed nervous as he huddled with the other guys. When he turned around he said, "Okay. This is a song I wrote for us. Check out our sound."

Artie, Phil, and Dwayne lined up with their backs to the sofa. Melody scooted forward, anxious for them to begin.

Dwayne started the tape recorder. They all spun around. *"Never thought I'd see the day that you made me feel this way,"* they sang together. *"Everything was sun, now everything is rain."*

Dwayne stepped forward. *"Never, ever dreamed you'd cause me this much pain."*

Melody smiled with pride. Big Momma said Dwayne's voice was a high tenor, like Smokey Robinson's. Melody thought Dwayne's singing was somehow even smokier.

At the last words, they all turned their backs to Melody and Lila again. The girls clapped and hooted and stomped their feet.

"Aw, come on!" Dwayne said happily, looking over his shoulder.

"We want a real critique," Phil said, smiling at Lila. Lila grinned back.

Melody noticed and leaned into her sister. "I thought you didn't like Phil," she whispered.

"He's turned kind of cute," Lila whispered back, adjusting her eyeglasses.

Melody shook her head. "What's the name of your group?" she asked the guys. "You need a catchy name."

"She's right," Lila said. "You're not still going by the name of 'Dwayne and The Detroiters,' are you?"

Dwayne looked sheepish. Artie pointed at Melody.

"Lil sis, you have a better idea?"

"Sure!" Melody thought for a moment. "How about The Three Ravens?" she suggested. "You could wear the same outfits, like The Temptations! Maybe black suits with matching purple shirts and ties—right, Lila?" Melody hopped up from her seat. "And those moves aren't cool enough. What if you spin one at a time—kind of bend and swirl around, like this?" Melody demonstrated. "When Dwayne is singing, you guys can't stand still," she said. "The Motown guys really dance."

Phil and Artie were already nodding, trying some different steps.

"Yeah! Yeah!" Melody nodded. "What do you think, Dwayne?"

"I'm thinking I can't believe how good you are at this, Dee-Dee," Dwayne said. "I'm going to get us some Kool-Aid," he said to the other two Ravens. Then he motioned for Melody to follow him to the kitchen.

Dwayne took down the pitcher, and Melody got out two packets of the strawberry powder and a wooden spoon.

"Here's the thing," Dwayne said. "Dad thinks I'm still working day shifts, but I quit my job at the factory."

"So that's why you're always coming and going!"

Dwayne nodded. "I got a part-time gig as a janitor down at Cobo Hall," he said. "Now I have more time to write music and rehearse with the guys."

Melody frowned. "Daddy's going to be really mad! You promised him you'd work at that factory until college started."

Dwayne shook his head. "I'm not cut out for

factory work, Dee-Dee. I got something good with
Phil and Artie, and we have a chance to make it great."
He turned on the water to fill the pitcher.

Melody looked down at the swirling red liquid.
Dwayne seemed so sure that he was right! Just like
Yvonne always did. Melody wished she had their kind
of courage.

"Listen," he said, turning back to her. "It's not
gonna be easy—I'm not fooling myself. But we can sell
records, lots of them. And I believe that when people
hear our sound, they won't care what color our skin is."

Melody hadn't known that was how Dwayne felt.
"Maybe if you explain that to Daddy, he'll understand.
I could tell him—"

"No!" Dwayne said quickly. "Promise you won't
say anything to Dad. We're gonna knock 'em out at our
audition. I just know it. Then I'll tell Mom and Dad."

Melody stirred the Kool-Aid slowly. "I'm not going
to tell a lie, you know."

"I know," Dwayne said, putting a hand on her
shoulder. "And I would never ask you to do that. Just
don't volunteer any information, okay?"

"I guess."

"There's one more thing," he said.

"What?" Melody set the spoon on the counter, and noticed that it was the same kind Dwayne had given her to drum on a pan a very long time ago.

"I need a new suit for the audition. Would you go shopping with me, since you seem to know just what I should be wearing?"

Melody couldn't help but smile. "All right," she said. "All right to everything, especially you telling Daddy soon. But—"

"But what?"

"Once I pick a song for Youth Day, you help me, too."

"You got it! Whatever you need." Dwayne picked up the spoon to continue stirring.

On Saturday morning, Dwayne and Melody ate Cheerios together and then got ready to go shopping. Big Momma always said, "Look like you have money in your pocket when you go into a store," so Dwayne brushed his hair and put on a shirt with a collar. Melody wore a school skirt and borrowed Lila's shoulder purse. She took two of the crisp one-dollar bills that she had gotten when she closed her account at the bank and tucked them into the purse. Melody told Dwayne she had decided to buy herself something special to wear for her solo at Youth Day. She was excited that they both had something to shop for.

Dwayne whistled a tune but didn't say much as they walked. A few blocks from home, they turned onto 12th Street, which was lined with shoe shops, dress stores, delicatessens, ice cream parlors, and all sorts of other businesses. On a Saturday morning, the sidewalk was crowded with shoppers. At one of the corners, Melody headed for the bus stop, but Dwayne kept walking.

"Hey!" Melody called out, dodging a lady with two little kids. "Where are we going?"

"Fieldston's," Dwayne said over his shoulder.

"I thought we were going downtown, to Hudson's department store," Melody said.

Dwayne made a face at her, and for a minute he looked more like a boy and not an almost grown-up man. "I don't have Hudson's money, Dee-Dee."

"Oh," Melody said. "I forgot. You're only working

part-time." Then she added, "We'll make it work!"

Fieldston's Clothing was one of the older stores on 12th Street. Poppa had often told them how he had bought his first city suit there when he moved up from Alabama. When he opened his flower shop several years later, there were only a few businesses owned by black people in the neighborhood. Even though Mr. Fieldston was white, he'd given Poppa lots of good advice. Now Mr. Fieldston was long gone, and someone else ran the store.

A bell chimed as Dwayne held the door open for Melody. There were three clerks chatting at the front counter, but none of them said, "May I help you?" or even "Hello." They were all wearing blue jackets, and they were all white. As she and Dwayne began to look around, Melody noticed several other shoppers, but she and her brother were the only black customers.

"The men's suits are over here," Dwayne said, nodding to the left. "But you'll want to see what's over there," he said, motioning to the right.

Melody saw a display of women's jewelry, and she smiled. "I'll just look for a few minutes," she told Dwayne. "Then I'll come and help you."

Melody hurried through the aisles crowded with clothing racks and display cases, her shoulder purse swinging. She stopped to admire some silky scarves. Melody wrapped one around her neck, turning to find a mirror so that she could see how she looked. She almost bumped into one of the clerks from the front of the store. "Excuse me," Melody said to the woman politely. The woman didn't say anything, but she watched as Melody took the scarf off and put it neatly back where she'd found it.

Melody wandered over to a glass case filled with necklaces. As she leaned closer, she saw the reflection of a man standing behind her. Thinking that he was looking too, she moved out of his way and on to a rack of barrettes. *Maybe I should get these instead of a headband,* she thought. She was about to take a pair from the rack when she changed her mind. She turned and saw the same man from the jewelry display. He looked at her suspiciously. Suddenly, Melody felt uncomfortable. She hurried over to Dwayne, no longer excited about shopping for herself.

Dwayne was holding up two black jackets. "How about one of these?" he asked.

"Oh! That's the one you need," Melody said, pointing to the one with the shiny gold buttons.

A young man came around the aisle carrying an armful of boxes. Dwayne held up the jacket with the shiny buttons. "Excuse me, what's the price on this?"

The man with the boxes gave Dwayne an annoyed look and brushed roughly past without answering. Dwayne shrugged and slipped the jacket on. Melody nodded her approval. It seemed to fit perfectly. Dwayne looked at the edge of the sleeve for a price tag, and then held his arm up high. "Can I get a price on this, please?"

"You can't afford it," a man said.

Melody turned to see the same man who'd stood behind her at the necklaces and the barrettes. Had he followed her?

"Take it off," the man said coldly.

"I have money," Dwayne said, frowning.

Melody looked toward the front counter. Mommy always said to ask nicely for a manager if you had trouble in a store.

The man shook his head, and Melody noticed that he was wearing the same blue jacket as all the other clerks. She suddenly suspected that he hadn't been standing behind her by mistake.

"I can guess what your kind really came in here for," he hissed.

"What do you mean?" Melody asked. "What's he talking about?" she whispered to Dwayne. Then she saw a look cross Dwayne's face—a look she'd never seen before. It was like anger and fear and something else all mixed together. Dwayne slowly took off the jacket and carefully hung it back on the rack, shaking his head.

"Wait," Melody said, tugging at her brother's arm. "You need a suit."

"Not at this price," Dwayne said quietly.

"I've had enough of your type," the clerk said. "Get out. And take your little shoplifting companion with you." His eyes flashed right at Melody.

"Shoplifting?" Melody's mouth dropped open. "That's not true," she protested. "We didn't steal any-thing," she said louder, her heart pounding. "We're just shopping like everybody else!"

"Dee-Dee, no." Dwayne didn't raise his voice. "Let's just go."

"You'd *better* go. Get out, before I call the cops!" the man shouted.

Melody realized with a sinking feeling that the man who was shouting was the manager. Dwayne was pulling her toward the door. She didn't want to stay, but she couldn't move. How could that man have accused her of doing something so horrible? As they left the store, Melody knew that Mommy had been wrong. That manager would never have helped them. He was the trouble.

Outside, Dwayne wouldn't look at Melody. He started walking so quickly that Melody had to almost run to keep up with him. She brushed away tears. Her insides were shaky, as if she'd just escaped something dangerous. Melody wanted to ask her brother if he was as upset as she was, and what he would do about his audition suit. "Dwayne?"

He spun around so quickly that she had to step back. His face was like a mask, as if he didn't feel anything at all.

"Should we go tell Poppa?" Melody asked.

Dwayne shook his head. "That won't help. Besides, this isn't the first time something like this has happened to me, and it won't be the last time."

Melody stood very still. Would that happen to her again? Would she be accused of shoplifting when she was just shopping? Then Melody felt a prickle of fear for her brother. What if the store clerk had called the police? Who would the police have believed, Dwayne or the clerk?

Melody took a deep breath. "Yvonne says we have to change things. That's why we have to march! That's why we're walking with Dr. King next Sunday."

Dwayne put his hand on Melody's shoulder. "I don't think a march is going to change things for me. Don't you see now? I have to use my talent to become a famous singer if I want things to be different."

Would people really treat Dwayne fairly if he was famous? Melody wondered. "I understand that you want to be famous," she said. "And I believe in you, Dwayne . . ."

"But?"

"But what about everyone else? Shouldn't we try to change things for people who aren't ever going to be famous? People who are just ordinary, like me?"

Dwayne cracked a half-smile. "Now you sound like Yvonne. The answer is yeah, everybody has to work to make things different. But we don't have to do it the same way. Everybody's got the power for change inside themselves. Music is mine."

Melody was shaken by what had happened in the store. But the idea that everybody had some great power inside made her feel more hopeful than she had just a few minutes ago.

"By the way, Dee-Dee," Dwayne said quietly, "you are not ordinary."

"I'm not?"

"Nothing close. I can't wait to see how you're gonna change the world, girl."

What Feels Right

*D*wayne walked Melody back home without talking much, and then he left to meet his friend Artie. Melody went inside. Mommy was the only one home, and she was talking on the telephone in the kitchen. The house was unusually quiet as Melody changed her clothes. She couldn't get the shouting manager out of her head, so she decided to go work in her garden. Being around plants and flowers always made her feel calm.

Life is such a puzzle, she thought as she weeded her flower bed. *How can some people be so unkind? If we all have the power to change things, why don't we?* Dwayne had told her that she would change the world. How could she, when she was having so much trouble picking out one song to sing?

Melody was in the backyard getting water from

the hose when she heard a car pull into the driveway. Val suddenly appeared around the corner of the house. "Val!" Melody said. "What are you doing here?"

"Do you want to go for a ride? Daddy and Mama want to check out some houses. Your mama said you can come, too."

Melody thought a fun outing might be nice after the way her morning one had turned out. She slipped off her gloves, tossed them onto the back steps, and followed Val.

Mommy was standing in the driveway, leaning toward the open window of the burgundy four-door Ford Fairlane. She was talking to Tish. "Well, I want to hear every detail of the house hunt when you get back!" Mommy said as Melody and Val climbed into the backseat. Charles tooted his horn twice and pulled away.

Cousin Tish turned to the girls from the front seat. "Now, y'all sit back. We're just doin' a cruise by some houses we saw listed in the newspaper. It'll be fun."

Melody nodded and pressed her head back against the soft seat. Tish turned the radio on. The DJ on the local station was reporting news about all the details of the freedom walk coming up in a week.

"Have you decided what you're going to sing for Youth Day yet?" Val asked, scooting close to Melody.

"How's that coming, honey?" Tish asked. "You know, your mama's so proud."

"I'm still trying to find a song that feels right," Melody said.

"That's sort of what we're doing today with houses, isn't it, Daddy?" Val said. "We're trying to find one that feels right."

"That's right, Princess," Charles replied.

At that moment, the radio announcer started talking about the songs that people might hear during the freedom walk. He mentioned "Lift Every Voice and Sing." Melody had always liked the title, and now, as the song began to play, she realized that it said what she was feeling inside. At that moment, Melody knew it was exactly what she wanted to sing for Youth Day.

Tish suddenly turned the volume down. "Oh, Charles, look!" she said, pointing to a house that was for sale.

"Mama, that yard is tiny," Val complained. "We need room for Melody to help me plant lots of flowers!"

"Okay, baby." Tish said. "We'll keep that in mind. We want all of us to be happy with our new home."

"Now, I like the brick houses in this neighborhood," Charles said, swinging onto a street lined with shade trees.

Both Melody and Val crowded to the same side of the car to peer out the window. The houses were all set back from the street on perfectly green lawns. Melody counted the trees spaced along the sidewalk, and marveled at the flower beds decorating nearly every yard.

"This is really nice," Tish murmured.

"There's a 'For Sale' sign up the street, Mama!" Val shouted.

"Let's get out and take a look," Charles said, cruising to a stop at the curb.

The house was pretty—like something Melody had seen in a magazine. It was two stories tall, a little smaller than her own house, and made of speckled light and dark red brick. There was a big picture window on one side of the green front door. The narrow roof was peaked, as if the house was wearing a pointy hat.

"I've been hoping for an upstairs!" Val whispered to

Melody. Melody smiled, remembering the fun she and
her sisters and brother had sliding down the upstairs
banister when her parents weren't looking.

Charles opened the car door for the girls, and Val
squeezed Melody's hand tightly as they followed the
adults along the walk and up the steps. Melody could
tell that Val was excited.

"I'll take down the real estate agent's name and
number from the sign," Tish said. She whipped out
a pen and a small notebook from her purse. "Hmm.
There's an open house tour next Sunday. You think we
can make it after church, honey?"

"I don't see why not," Charles said.

Melody had hoped that Charles and Tish would
change their minds and join the rest of the family at the
freedom walk next week, but it didn't sound as if they
would.

All four of them peered into the big front window.
The house was empty, and they could see straight
through to part of the kitchen.

"It's got a fireplace," Tish said, scribbling in her
notebook. "I've always wanted a fireplace, Charles."

Val nudged Melody. "Let's see what the backyard

looks like!" she said. The girls raced around the house, but there was a high fence on the side and across the back. All they could see was the top of a skinny tree.

"I had a swing set back in Birmingham," Val sighed. "Daddy says I can have one here, too."

Melody was looking up at the house next door. "Hey! Somebody's looking at us," she said, stepping back from the fence between the yards. Melody smiled and waved, and Val joined her. The woman in the window did not wave back. Instead, she pulled the curtains closed.

"What was that about?" Val asked as they wandered back to the front yard.

"I don't know, but it was weird," Melody said.

Val's parents were standing at the curb, and Tish was taking pictures with a camera.

"This is what I'm looking for," Charles said. "A quiet neighborhood where a man can enjoy his home without any troubles."

"All right, y'all, this one is on my list," Tish said. "Let's keep going!" Her high heels clicked on the walk as she headed back to the car.

"It's on the *top* of my list," Charles said. He turned

to the girls, who were lagging behind. "What do you think, Val?"

"I like it a lot, Daddy!"

"Melody," Cousin Charles asked, "is there sufficient flower-planting space for your liking?"

"Yes, sir," Melody answered. She and Val giggled as they climbed into the car. When Melody looked at the house next door, she saw the blinds in a downstairs window flutter.

Tish flipped the radio on just in time for them to hear a voice singing, *"My mama told me, you better shop around!"*

"Well, how do you like that!" she said with a laugh. "Even Smokey Robinson is giving us advice!"

Charles drove them around Detroit for another hour, and they saw dozens of other houses for sale. But everyone agreed that they liked the pointy-hat house the most.

"Let's head on home," Tish said. "I'll fix some lunch."

Charles nodded. "And I'll call the real estate agent."

When they arrived at Melody's grandparents' house, there was the sound of music coming from the open windows. Inside, Big Momma paused her piano playing to give everyone big hugs. "How was the house hunting?" she asked.

"We saw the nicest place!" Tish opened her purse, took out her notebook, and handed it to Charles.

"I'll make the call upstairs," he said. "Do you mind, Big Momma?"

"You go right ahead, honey," she said.

"Help me out with lunch, Valerie," Tish said, heading for the kitchen.

Val followed her mother, and Big Momma turned back to the piano. She started playing a tune softly, and that reminded Melody of the song from the car radio.

"Big Momma, could you play 'Lift Every Voice and Sing'?" Melody asked. She wasn't surprised when her grandmother stopped the song she had been playing and seamlessly started "Lift Every Voice." Big Momma didn't need any sheet music.

"Many people call this the Negro National Anthem," Big Momma said as she played. "A colored man, James Weldon Johnson, wrote the lyrics as a poem, and his brother wrote the music."

"What are the lyrics?" Melody asked. She had listened to the song many times, but now she wanted to hear all the words.

Big Momma stopped playing. "I have the music right here," she said. She stood and opened her piano bench and looked through several sheets of music. Then she handed Melody an old songbook.

"Lift every voice and sing, till earth and heaven ring." Melody read the first line and imagined being able to sing out, loud and strong, so the whole world could hear.

"Would you play it again, please?" Melody asked.

Big Momma sat down again. Melody propped the book on the piano and then stood close to Big Momma, reading the words silently as she followed the music. When the song ended, Melody felt the most wonderful feeling stirring inside her.

"Just in case you need to know," Big Momma whispered, "no one has ever sung this at a Youth Day concert before."

The Walk to Freedom

♪ CHAPTER 11 ♩

*m*elody couldn't get the tune of "Lift Every Voice and Sing" out of her mind. She'd carried around the songbook Big Momma had given her all week. She'd memorized all three verses, and on the afternoon of the freedom walk, she was thinking hard about the words.

"Yvonne," Melody asked, "what does it mean to *ring with the harmonies of liberty*?" She could see her sister's face in the mirror over the dresser. Yvonne finished smoothing Melody's hair before she answered.

"Harmony is everybody joining together."

"You mean, playing nicely, like Mommy used to tell us?"

"Right. And liberty—"

"Means free. I know. Like the Pledge of Allegiance."

"That's a really important song you're learning,

Dee-Dee," Yvonne told her, adjusting Melody's headband.

"Why?"

"Well . . ." Yvonne wrinkled her face in thought. "It's about the future, really. I mean, most black Americans are relatives of people who were brought to this country in chains. Slavery went on for two hundred and fifty years. And even though last January was the one hundreth anniversary of the Emancipation Proclamation that outlawed slavery, black people today are still being oppressed."

Melody spun around from her chair. "Oppressed?"

"It means held back. You know, not allowed to shop where they want or get the jobs they want or live where they want. Not allowed to really be free."

Yvonne put Melody's brush down on the dresser and picked up the big, fork-like comb that she used for her Afro. "So, see?" she continued. "This song encourages us to remember how strong we were in the past, but also pushes us to keep being strong now, to keep fighting every day until—"

"—*until earth and heaven ring*." Melody said. She was beginning to understand. "And that means never giving up until everything is fair, doesn't it?"

Yvonne patted Melody on her shoulders and said, "Liberty and justice is for all, little sis. That's why kids in the South march, that's why I help folks register to vote, and that's why we're walking in Detroit today."

Melody thought back to how the man at Fieldston's had treated her and Dwayne so unfairly. Melody wanted the Walk to Freedom to keep things like that from happening in the future.

"Melody," Daddy called up the stairs. "It's time to go."

"What about you?" Melody asked Yvonne.

"I'm riding with friends," Yvonne explained. "I'll be walking with some other college students. You'd better hurry down."

Daddy drove Melody, Lila, and Mommy in the station wagon to pick up Poppa and Big Momma. As Melody watched her grandparents hurrying to the car, she realized that they were both frowning.

"What happened?" Mommy asked Big Momma when they had settled into the station wagon.

"Tish and Charles drove all the way out to that open house today—"

Melody chimed in from the fold-down seat. "The pointy-hat house, Big Momma? The brick one?"

"Yes. They got there, and the real estate agent told them the open house was cancelled."

Poppa made a "harrumph" sound.

"Where was the house located, exactly?" Mommy asked. When Big Momma told her, Mommy shook her head. Melody could see a flash of anger in Daddy's eyes through the rearview mirror.

Melody was confused. "What happened?" she asked.

"That neighborhood has been in the news lately," Poppa said. "Several home owners have done the same thing. I'll bet somebody doesn't want colored—black—neighbors. So if a black couple shows up, the agent cancels the appointment, or the owner decides not to sell to them."

"That's wrong!" Lila said.

"It *is* wrong," Poppa told her, "but it's not illegal. It should be against the law to keep colored folks from buying any home they can afford."

Melody thought about the woman she and Val had seen in the windows of the house next to the pointy-hat house. Could that woman, who had been white, have told the real estate agent to keep Val's family away? "Charles and Tish should come to the march," Melody said. "To protest."

"They never planned to walk," Poppa reminded them.

"That's a shame," Mommy said, "because one of the reasons for this walk is to call for fair housing laws."

Everyone was quiet. Melody stared out the window thinking about how disappointed Val and Tish and Charles must be. They had all been so excited about that house. Melody felt a little like a balloon whose air was leaking out.

As they drove along Woodward, Melody saw hundreds of people heading downtown on foot.

"This is like going to the Hudson's Thanksgiving Day parade," Lila said. "Look at the crowds!"

Melody perked up. She saw some people carrying flags and others waving signs that looked just like the ones she and Lila had helped make.

"This traffic is something awful," Poppa said. "Will, maybe we'd better park the car and start walking already." Daddy didn't argue. He pulled over at the next empty spot near a curb.

"I see a group from New Bethel Baptist Church," Mommy said. "Reverend C. L. Franklin is pastor there. He helped organize the walk and bring Dr. King to speak." She stopped to tie a scarf over her hair and put on sunglasses.

"I hear a band," Lila said.

Melody strained to hear, but the music was too far away for her to recognize the tune. She looked up at the clear blue sky, and at the crowd gathering from all the side streets. This was different from a parade.

Daddy opened the back of the station wagon and pulled out two neatly lettered signs. One said "Down with Discrimination." The other read "Justice Now."

"That's the one I made," Melody said proudly.

Lila grabbed it. "I can hold it higher," she said.

Melody pouted, but she knew Lila was right. Daddy lifted the other sign high above everyone's heads.

"I believe there are thousands of folks out here," Mommy said as she took Melody's hand.

Poppa nodded. "More than they predicted on the radio."

Cobo Hall was the biggest auditorium in Detroit,

built right near the Detroit River. People flowed slowly toward Cobo as if they had become a river, and the river sang.

Melody listened. She knew the song, and she opened her mouth to join in, just as Big Momma did, too. Together they sang

> *We shall not,*
> *We shall not be moved.*
> *We shall not,*
> *We shall not be moved.*
> *Just like a tree that's standing by the water,*
> *We shall not be moved.*

Big Momma took Melody's other hand. Walking there, between her mother and her grandmother, raising her girl voice with theirs, Melody felt strangely light, as if she could fly if they let go of her hands. And all the other voices surrounding them were like hearts, beating together. *This is harmony*, Melody thought.

The sea of bodies slowed even more, and then stopped. Melody couldn't see Cobo Hall, but she knew they were still far away from the entrance.

Mommy let go of Melody and took out her camera to snap pictures. "This is even more remarkable than I expected," Mommy said.

"I wish Val were here," Melody said to Mommy. "And Dwayne." Dwayne had made good on his promise not to join them and had gone to Artie's after church.

"I know, sweetheart," Mommy said, taking Melody's hand again. "You'll have to listen hard. Then you can tell Val all about it."

"This is as close as we're going to get," Poppa said.

"At least we'll be able to hear the speeches," Daddy said. "They've got speakers set up."

The speakers crackled, and the singing faded. A man said something over the loudspeaker, and then someone else spoke. Melody's legs began to get tired, and she wondered when Dr. King would preach.

Then the roar of applause rose around them. Melody heard a different man's voice, a strong, clear, Southern voice. At last it was Dr. King! He talked about Abraham Lincoln, and the Emancipation Proclamation that freed Negroes from slavery. He talked about Birmingham, and how racial segregation was wrong.

Melody didn't understand everything Dr. King said, but she felt the excitement of the crowds around her as they shouted out "Yes!" at certain parts of his speech. People clapped and cheered so hard at other times that Dr. King had to pause. His words took on a rhythm, and he was almost chanting.

"I have a dream," he said. "With this faith I will go out with you and transform dark yesterdays into bright tomorrows . . ." Melody's insides began to shiver as she thought of the words to "Lift Every Voice":

> Sing a song, full of the faith
> > that the dark past has taught us

All of her family's stories flashed through Melody's mind: Poppa leaving his farm, Mommy making the triple-chocolate cake because Daddy couldn't buy one, Yvonne being turned away at the bank, Dwayne being treated badly at Fieldston's.

> Sing a song full of the hope
> > that the present has brought us

Poppa had moved to Detroit and opened his flower shop—where Yvonne now had a summer job. Now Mommy made the best cake ever, and Dwayne was determined to succeed in a music career so that he would be treated fairly. None of them had ever given up hope. Melody felt inspired.

Dr. King was chanting, "Free at last! Free at last!" The applause was like thunder in the sunshine.

On the walk back to the car, Melody made an announcement. "For Youth Day, I'm going to do 'Lift Every Voice and Sing.'"

"That's a big song for you, Little One!" Poppa said with a smile. She saw Mommy nodding her approval.

"Yes, it is," Melody said to him. "But when I hear it, I feel the way I did listening to Dr. King. That's how I want the audience to feel when I sing at Youth Day. Dwayne says when the words mean something special to a singer, amazing things happen."

Daddy looked at her with surprise as he unlocked the station wagon. "Dwayne said that, did he?"

"Isn't that the song that you've been humming in

your sleep?" Lila asked, climbing into the folding seat.

"I guess," Melody said, noticing that her grand-mother hadn't said a word. "Do you think it's a good fit, Big Momma?" Melody whispered.

Big Momma gave Melody's hand a squeeze. "Your brother is right. And I believe my chick can do any-thing she sets her mind to."

Lila snapped her fingers. "Make it work, Dee-Dee. Make it work!"

Val was watching from the front window when they returned from the march. She threw open Big Momma's front door and ran out. "How was it? Did you carry my sign? Did you see Dr. King?"

"It was great! And no, and no!" Melody answered with enthusiasm. "Lila carried your sign, and we didn't get close enough to see Dr. King, but we heard him." Melody took a breath. "But are you okay? Poppa told us what happened with the house."

Val's shoulders drooped. "It makes me sad to think that it could have been our house. Mama was sad at first, too, but now she's mad."

Melody didn't want Val to give up her hopes of a swing set and an upstairs. She remembered something from the Walk to Freedom. "Dr. King said he has a dream that black people in Detroit will be able to buy the houses they want," Melody told her cousin.

"Really?" Val asked. "Dr. King said that?"

"Mm-hmm." Melody smiled, looping her arm through her cousin's. "Things are going to change. I just know it."

Fireworks

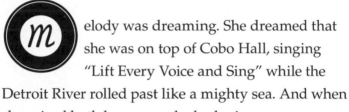elody was dreaming. She dreamed that she was on top of Cobo Hall, singing "Lift Every Voice and Sing" while the Detroit River rolled past like a mighty sea. And when she raised both her arms, she had wings.

She woke up, and for a few seconds, she thought she might still be dreaming. She smelled dinner instead of breakfast. Then she heard the low rumbling of men's voices outside, and sniffed the wisps of hickory smoke wafting through the open window. It was the Fourth of July. Daddy had the entire day off from work, and Melody knew he was up already, tending the barbecue. She squinted over at Lila and Yvonne, who were both still asleep, and then at the Mickey Mouse alarm clock. Mickey's hands pointed to six o'clock.

Melody hurried to get dressed, wondering what

time Val was coming over. She didn't stop to put on her shoes, and instead ran downstairs barefoot with Bo at her heels. She swung around the stair post at the end of the banister, saw a pink bundle curled up on the sofa, and almost tripped on the rug.

"Val!" Melody shouted, and Bo barked excitedly. "Shhh!" Melody frowned at him when she remembered how early it was.

Val sat up, blinking her sleepy eyes. Bo rushed over to her. "Hey, doggy." Val scratched between his ears and yawned at Melody. "My daddy came over to help your daddy, and I came along. How is your song coming?"

Melody had told Val that the Walk to Freedom had helped her pick her song for Youth Day. "I know all the words, but I have to start working on the music."

"My mama says 'Lift Every Voice and Sing' is beautiful, but it's not easy to sing." Val absentmindedly began to pat down her messy hair.

"Here, let me!" Melody said. She sat next to Val and parted her cousin's hair with her fingers, making two careful braids. "Big Momma says things worth having don't come easy."

"I wish she'd tell that to Mama and Daddy again," Val said. "Now they can't agree on where we're gonna live. I never knew it was so hard to buy a house."

"I know they'll make it work," Melody said.

Val pulled away to look at her and laugh. "You say that all the time!"

"That's because my mother does. Come on. Let's go see what the daddies are doing outside."

Melody, Val, and Bo sped through the dining room and burst into the kitchen. Melody didn't expect her mother to be up yet, so she was surprised to see Mommy wearing her red-white-and-blue-striped blouse and dancing to the radio.

"Happy Fourth of July, girls!" Mommy said. She was holding a bowl full of lemons that had been cut in half. "You're just in time to start the lemonade! Daddy put the big crock outside on the picnic table." She handed Val the bowl and Melody a juicer.

Melody looked at the mound of lemons. "Are there a lot of people coming over?"

Mommy spoke over her shoulder from the kitchen sink. "The family, Miss Esther from the church, a few of Yvonne's friends, and Dwayne's friends Phil and

Artie. You and Val can be a big help to me."

Melody crossed the cool linoleum of the kitchen,
pushed the back door open, and held it for Val. Daddy
heard it creak and waved his tongs. Melody smiled.
No matter how late her father worked on the day before
the Fourth of July, he was always standing at his grill
as soon as the sun came up.

Cousin Charles was wearing the baggiest shorts
that Melody had ever seen. She held back a giggle.

"Aren't Daddy's shorts the ugliest?" Val leaned her
chin on Melody's shoulder.

"Yep," Melody laughed. The girls got to work,
taking turns juicing the lemons.

Charles was busy setting up folding tables and
chairs around the yard. "Dee-Dee, I heard you're going
to sing today!"

"I kind of told Daddy you would," Val said.

Melody shook her head. "Not my Youth Day song,
but we can still sing." Then she had an idea. "Let's put
on a show!" Melody said to Val. "You and Lila and I
could pretend to be The Vandellas or The Marvelettes."

"That's a great idea!" Val said.

"We've got one of Big Momma's old microphones

upstairs, and I bet Yvonne would help us dress up."

"Do you think Lila will sing?" Val asked doubtfully.

"Oh, I think so," Melody giggled. If Dwayne's friend Phil was going to be in the audience, she was pretty sure Lila would agree to be part of the act.

Mommy came out to help the girls finish the lemonade, and then gave them ears of corn to shuck. Afterward, Melody got her gardening gloves.

"I need to do some weeding," Melody said to Val. "Do you want to help?"

"You mean, dig in dirt?"

Melody laughed. "Sure. The flowers that make our neighborhood look nice grow in dirt. The tomatoes we're going to eat today grew in this dirt. I love growing things as much as I love to sing. Sometimes I sing to my plants, too."

"You do?" Val thought that was funny. "Sure, I'll help. But I've never weeded a garden before." Val borrowed a pair of Melody's gardening gloves, and the two of them knelt between the neat rows of cabbages and greens.

"This is kind of fun," Val said after they'd been pulling and singing. "I think I might like a garden of my own—if we ever get our own place."

"You will," Melody assured her. "And I'll help you make it bloom."

"Hey, you girls have that garden looking like something from a magazine!" Charles called.

Val nodded. "Melody's a real gardener, Daddy!"

"Well the work goes much faster with four hands instead of two," Melody laughed.

When the vegetable garden and flower beds were weeded, Val cleaned up in the bathroom and Melody went to the bedroom she shared with her sisters.

Yvonne was already downstairs, but Lila was still in bed. She rolled over and groaned when Melody slammed a drawer.

"Are you awake, Lila?"

Lila opened one eye. "What time is it? Why are you making so much noise?"

"Sorry. It's nine o'clock. Would you put on a show with Val and me later, when everyone comes over? We'll be The Marvelettes!"

Lila closed her eyes again.

"Mommy says Phil will be here," Melody added.

Lila's eyes popped open and Melody skipped out

of their room. Val was waiting in the hall, grinning because she'd overheard the conversation.

"I think Lila will sing with us," Melody said. The girls giggled as they hurried down the steps.

Around two in the afternoon Poppa, Big Momma, and Tish arrived. Soon after, Yvonne's friends began to fill in the backyard. One of them was a young man from Ghana who was studying in Detroit. Melody was fascinated by his beautiful robes, which he said he wore "in honor of this Independence Day." Dwayne, Artie, and Phil cornered him near the back steps and asked him all about African music.

Melody and Val were playing jacks in the driveway when Melody looked up to see Miss Esther tapping her cane along the concrete. She was carrying a plate wrapped in wax paper.

Melody scrambled up. "I can take that for you, Miss Esther," Melody said, reaching for the plate. She wanted to peek at what was under the paper, but didn't.

"Tea cakes," Miss Esther told her.

Melody smiled. "Everybody's in the backyard," she said. "I'll walk you around."

"And I'll carry the tea cakes," Val said, taking the plate from Melody and heading up the driveway.

Miss Esther nodded, but instead of following Val, she stood looking at the Ellisons' yard. "I just want to take a minute to admire these lovely flower beds," Miss Esther said. "Your mother must spend a lot of time keeping them up."

"No, ma'am. I do it," Melody said proudly.

"*You* do? What an eye for color you have! I notice every time I drive by. You know, beautiful plants and flowers can change more than the look of a neighborhood. They can change the way a place feels, too."

"Do you have a garden?" Melody asked as she and Miss Esther strolled along the driveway.

"I used to," Miss Esther replied. "But I don't anymore." She stopped and pointed her cane along the side of the house. "Tell me about what you have planted here. And here!"

It took Melody and Miss Esther almost half an hour to make it to the backyard. They walked slowly and talked about Melody's flowers and the garden Miss Esther used to have and how much they both liked to plant things and watch them grow.

"There's nothing better than seeing a tiny bud bloom into something beautiful," Miss Esther said as they joined the party. "You know that too, don't you, Melody?"

"Yes, ma'am," Melody agreed.

Melody's mother came over to greet Miss Esther and show her to a chair under the big shade tree. Val raced across the yard and grabbed Melody's arm. "I thought you'd never get back here."

"Miss Esther is one of the most interesting grown-ups I've ever met," Melody said. "We were talking about gardens. She knows as much about growing things as Poppa."

Val grinned. "I didn't think that was possible." Then she tugged Melody's arm. "Come on. Yvonne's going to help us get ready for our number."

As the girls headed toward the back door, Dwayne was pulling a bottle of Vernor's Ginger Ale out of a big tub full of ice. "Hey, Dee-Dee," he called. "You didn't ask me to join your group!"

Melody laughed. "It's just us *girls*. Do you want to be our stagehand?"

"Sure—whatever you need." He made a funny bow.

When Melody and Val got upstairs, Yvonne and one of her girlfriends were piling her bed with some of the dresses Yvonne had outgrown. Lila was fussing with the old microphone. "I hope this thing works," she muttered. "Somebody find me a screwdriver!"

Val sifted through the dresses on the bed. "I like this one!" she said, grabbing a blue dress. "And look at this, Dee-Dee! It's perfect for you!" Val held up a flowered dress with a bow at the waist.

Melody couldn't believe her eyes. "Can I really wear that one, Vonnie?" Yvonne hadn't worn the dress for years, but she hadn't ever let Lila or Melody wear it, either.

"For today," Yvonne answered. "Yes."

"Which Marvelettes song should we do?" Melody asked, holding the dress up in front of her. It was a little bit big, but they could pin it if they needed to.

"How about 'Please Mr. Postman'?" Yvonne suggested, sweeping Melody's hair up on top of her head. "You girls sing that all the time."

Val was tipping awkwardly in a pair of Yvonne's high heels. *"C'mon, deliver the letter, the sooner the better,"* she sang as Yvonne poked Melody's hair with bobby pins.

Once the older girls finished pinning and piling hair and buttoning and zipping dresses, Melody, Val, and Lila each twirled in front of the full-length mirror. Melody couldn't help grinning at what she saw. They weren't wearing matching dresses, but they still looked like Motown stars!

The girls hurried down to the kitchen, where they waited for Dwayne to hush the crowd in the backyard. "Ladies and gentlemen," Dwayne announced as the girls and their dresses floated onto the back stoop. "Introducing the Even More Marvelous Marvelettes!"

Val giggled at the name Dwayne had invented, and Lila made sure the microphone worked. Melody fidgeted with the bow on her dress, but she wasn't one bit nervous. Already the music was inside her head, and her feet began to move.

"Music!" Lila ordered.

Dwayne and his bandmates started doo-wopping the song, and Melody, Val, and Lila began singing.

Melody put her heart into having a good time. By the end of the song, she was dancing and waving her arms along with Val and Lila. Other people were dancing, too, including her parents, Charles and Tish, and even Poppa and Big Momma.

"Encore!" Dwayne yelled when they finished. "That means one more time!" They sang the song again, and everyone in the backyard joined in.

Finally breathless, Melody and Val collapsed on the steps. Tish handed each of them a cold bottle of Vernor's.

"That was so much fun," Val said.

"I am starved!" Lila gasped, biting into a hot dog. "You'd better get one. Dad says he's running out of charcoal."

Val shook her head, but Melody headed for the grill. Her father pressed a plump hot dog into a bun and handed it to Melody. "Nice job, daughter," he said, smiling. "I know you'll do the same on Youth Day."

"Thanks, Daddy."

He wiped sweat from his forehead and handed Charles his long grilling fork. "This crowd is still hungry. If you man the grill, I'll go for more charcoal."

"You got it," Charles agreed.

"I'm hot!" Val said when Melody returned to the back steps. "Let's go out front and see if there's a cooler breeze."

The girls were on the front porch, and Melody had just finished her hot dog, when Daddy returned. When he got out of the car, her father slammed the door so hard that both girls stared. "Is your brother still here?" he said in a low voice.

Melody nodded her head. "Yes, Daddy."

Her father didn't even get the charcoal out of the back of the wagon. He stomped past them and into the backyard.

"What happened?" Val asked.

"I think something bad," Melody said, the fun of the day fading. She heard Daddy yelling for Dwayne. The entire neighborhood could probably hear him yelling. The back door opened and closed, and Melody heard Dwayne and her parents in the living room.

Melody told Val, "I'll be back," and went inside.

"I just ran into Joe Walker at the store," Daddy was saying. "He says you're a part-time janitor at Cobo Hall. He says you work a few hours in the afternoons. I want to know how you can be a day janitor at Cobo Hall when you're working a day shift at the factory."

Dwayne dropped his head for a beat. "I'm not working at the factory anymore, Dad."

"What?" Mommy said. She sounded shocked.

Dwayne sighed. "I quit the factory a while ago. I needed more time for writing and rehearsing, and—"

"Rehearsing!" Daddy said angrily. "Boy, what is wrong with you? You know how hard it is for a Negro to get his foot in the door at that factory? You could have a steady job every summer when you're home from school!"

"Dad, I don't want my foot in that door." Dwayne wasn't shouting. He was calm. "I don't want to work at the factory. I don't want to go to college. I want a music career!"

"Daddy, he's really good," Melody said.

Their father seemed not to hear. Mommy put a hand on Melody's shoulder.

"You promised us that you'd work at the factory and then go to college," Mommy said.

"I'm sorry, Dad. Mom. I can't keep that promise. I've got an audition at Motown next Thursday with my band. This is my chance. I have to try."

Daddy narrowed his eyes as he stood almost nose to nose with Dwayne. They were the same height. They had the same chin. Melody held her breath. To her surprise, it wasn't her father who spoke first.

"I'll pack my stuff," Dwayne said.

Melody exchanged a worried glance with her mother.

"I didn't ask—" Daddy didn't finish.

Dwayne put one hand on his father's shoulder and looked directly at him. "I know you didn't, Dad. But if Mr. Gordy likes us, he'll send us on the road right away to see how we perform for real audiences. I'll go stay at Phil's." He held out his other hand for a handshake.

Daddy looked down at Dwayne's hand, then back at his face. In slow motion, he shook Dwayne's hand.

Dwayne looked at Mommy. "I can't be somebody I'm not," he said. "I'll make it work, Mom." Dwayne turned on his heel and bounded up the stairs.

Daddy looked at Mommy, and then at Melody. He seemed to notice her for the first time. "You say he's good?"

"Yes, Daddy," Melody whispered.

"Will, I don't go along with this notion of skipping college," Mommy said quietly. "But Melody's right. He's very, very good."

Daddy shook his head. "He'd better be. If he thinks factory work is hard, wait until he learns what that music business is like. I know some fellows who tried going down that road. It was too tough, and they couldn't make it."

Melody's parents went to the kitchen, talking and talking all the way outside. *Dwayne will make it work,* Melody told herself, trying not to cry. She sat on the bottom stair to make sure her brother didn't leave without saying good-bye. He didn't take long to come down.

"Melody, look. I didn't mean for things to happen like this."

Melody bit her lip. "Will you ever come home again?"

"If you're trying to tell me good-bye, forget it, sis," Dwayne said. "I'm gonna keep turning up, when you least expect me."

Melody looked down at her toes. "You won't be here to help me get ready for Youth Day."

"I'm sorry about that. You don't really need me, though. Big Momma has you covered. You listen to her. You'll be all right." He stood up. "I gotta go. Tell the sister-things I'll catch them later. And be good."

As soon as Dwayne had gone and closed the door behind him, the house felt different to Melody. She closed her eyes and listened. In the kitchen, the news was droning on her mother's radio. Outside, voices mingled with Bo's barking. Something had changed, though. Without Dwayne's humming or singing in the background to all those sounds, her family was off-key.

In a few minutes, Lila and Yvonne came in.

"What happened?" Lila asked.

"Dad looked really mad," Yvonne said. "So we didn't dare ask him anything."

Melody told them everything.

"Well, it *is* Independence Day," Lila said. "What better day for Dwayne to go out on his own? Right, Vonnie?"

"Face it," Yvonne said, "Dwayne is hardheaded. Sooner or later, he would have quit the factory. Dwayne lives and breathes music. I know Daddy wasn't happy, but how could he be surprised?"

Melody thought about the expressions on her parents' faces. They were surprised all right. And hurt.

Lila and Yvonne went back out, but Melody didn't feel like rejoining the party. She sat inside for a long time. By the time she went back outside, the sun had set. Miss Esther was gone, and her parents were talking to Yvonne and her friends. Her grandparents were sitting side by side under the tree in the deepening dark of dusk.

"If you're looking for Val and Lila, Charles took them to the fireworks," Poppa said. Big Momma motioned for Melody to come over to them. Melody sat on the grass near their knees.

"How are you feeling about your brother?" Big Momma asked.

"Kind of down," Melody said.

"Dwayne needs growing-into-a-man space," Poppa said. "He has to leave home to find it."

Big Momma said, "One day, you'll need growing-into-a-woman space, and you'll leave home too. It's what we all do."

Melody twisted her neck to look up. "Did you?"

Big Momma chuckled. "Yes, I did. Dorothy and I

went on the road as gospel singers, remember?"

"Oh, yes."

"It's time, chick."

Melody nearly choked as she swallowed a gulp of ginger ale. "Time for *me*?"

"Time for you to grow. Time to lift that beautiful instrument of yours. We'll start on Monday. Ten o'clock sharp."

Practice

n the Monday after the Fourth of July, Melody was at her grandparents' house at exactly 9:59 a.m.

"Valerie," Big Momma said, "I'm afraid you can't sit in on Melody's session. She needs to concentrate. Go on in the kitchen, darlin'."

Val faked a wide-eyed, fearful expression, then winked at Melody and scurried into the other room. Val's goofiness made Melody smile, even though she was actually nervous.

"Let's do a few warm-up exercises, all right?" Big Momma sat on the piano bench and began to play scales. Melody stood beside the piano with her back straight and her arms at her sides. She hummed to match the notes that Big Momma played. When Melody's voice was ready, they moved on to her Youth Day song.

Melody had sung only a few lines when they were interrupted by a furious knocking at the door. When Big Momma stopped playing and got up to answer it, Melody was surprised to see Diane Harris.

"Mrs. Porter! My mother got my lesson time mixed up, and she's on a double shift, and my dad dropped me off, and—" Diane's frantic explanation squeaked to a halt when she noticed Melody. The girls stared at each other for a moment.

"Mistakes happen, Diane," Big Momma said. "You'll have your lesson after Melody's. Come on in and pass right through to the kitchen. Melody's cousin Valerie is there, and you can sit with her. I need y'all to be as quiet as possible."

Big Momma sat back down at the piano as if nothing had happened. "Let's start at the beginning. Key?" Big Momma played a note, and Melody adjusted her voice by singing "Ahhh."

"Good. Here we go." She played.

Melody exhaled, thinking of the Walk to Freedom and how inspired she'd been after hearing Dr. King speak. She wanted people to feel the same way when they heard her sing this song.

She sang the entire first verse, but she didn't always hit the right notes. It was hard to keep up with the tempo because of the way the music swooped up and down, especially in the middle. Melody anxiously watched her grandmother's face for a sign of how she was doing.

Big Momma stopped playing. "Again," she said. "From the beginning."

For half an hour, Melody sang. Big Momma stopped frequently to give Melody direction. Melody had to sing one line over and over again. Finally, Big Momma closed her music book.

"Good," she said. Melody's heart thumped. Big Momma hadn't said "Excellent!" or "Wonderful." Just "Good." Melody waited.

"We have to work on tempo. That's every singer's challenge with this song. Your lyrics aren't quite keeping pace with the music. And you have to make your voice sound bigger."

Melody nodded. "Lifting it, you mean. I'll work hard, I promise." She meant it.

Big Momma handed Melody a cassette tape. On the

case, written in Big Momma's scratchy handwriting, were the words: "For Melody's Practice."

"I made you this tape recording yesterday so you will have music to work with at home," Big Momma said. "You've given yourself a real challenge, my chick. And I know you'll conquer it. Now, enough. Wednesday, we'll do it again."

Melody twirled herself to the kitchen door, only remembering as she pushed it open that Diane was there.

"That was the Negro National Anthem," Diane said. "Are you singing that for Youth Day?" She looked surprised. "I never knew you could sound so good," she said, pushing her way past Melody and through the kitchen door.

Melody was speechless. *Did Diane just compliment my voice?* Melody looked at Val. "What did you say to her?"

Val laughed. "It wasn't anything I said. It was what you sang, Dee-Dee."

On Thursday evening, Melody and her sisters were

waiting anxiously to hear about Dwayne's audition. Mommy was still at a church meeting when the phone finally rang around nine o'clock. Melody jumped off the sofa, but Yvonne got to the phone first. Dwayne asked to speak to their father. Daddy had worked a full day's shift and was asleep already, but Yvonne went to wake him up.

Melody and Lila hurried up the stairs after her and huddled outside their parents' bedroom with Yvonne, listening.

"Say what?" Daddy said. He sounded sleepy.

"I'm not so sure it was a good idea to wake him up," Lila said, poking Yvonne with her elbow.

"Is he even going to remember talking?" Melody asked.

Yvonne put her finger to her lips. "Shh! Listen!"

"Yeah?" Daddy sounded a bit more awake. "No kidding? So what do they pay you for that? What? You would've done better on the assembly line. I'm going to sleep." There was a pause and then Daddy said, "You watch yourself out there. And call your mother." Daddy slammed the phone down. "All you sisters! Your brother is working for Motown. Good night!" In a very few minutes, Daddy was snoring as loud as the car engines he helped build at the Ford factory.

"I can't believe it," Yvonne said. "Dwayne is making his dream come true."

"You think Daddy is still mad at him?" Melody asked.

Lila yawned. "He didn't sound like it." She took off her eyeglasses and cleaned them with the edge of her shirt.

Yvonne made a clucking sound at her. "You need to take a break from studying. You're going to wear your eyes out."

"I have one chance to get into this school," Lila said. "I'm not going to mess it up."

"Of course you won't." Yvonne stood up. "How about some cookies and milk to feed your big brain? We can celebrate for Dwayne. Then you can go to bed and wake up to a new day with your books."

Lila laughed, and Melody had to smile. As the girls headed to the kitchen, Melody found herself humming and singing in her head: *Facing the rising sun of our new day begun, let us march on till victory is won.*

Mommy got a short note from Dwayne soon after his call, telling her that The Three Ravens were touring with a few other groups. Melody got a postcard of New Orleans from him that only said, "Everything going real good. Thought I saw Sharon running by the stage. Ha, Ha! Dwayne."

Melody was glad that her brother was getting to perform, but home didn't quite feel like home without him. Other things were also changing. Mommy taught summer school four days a week, so she wasn't around to take Melody to the movies or to the soda fountain at Barthwell's. Yvonne spent most of her time either working at the flower shop or at meetings of the Student Walk to Freedom club she'd started. Lila was closed up in their room or at the library preparing for her test at the end of August. She was so snappy now that Melody only said "Hi" and "Bye" to her. Melody felt like the harmony her family had always shared was missing. She wondered how they could make it sound right again.

Melody was grateful that Val was close by, even

though it meant that her parents hadn't found their new house yet. Tish *had* found a space for her new salon, though, and she was busy getting ready to open.

One day at the end of July, Melody and Val were in Big Momma's kitchen arranging flowers in a vase. The sounds of a halting piano lesson came from the living room. "Diane?" Val asked.

Melody nodded. "She's getting better."

"A little," Val agreed, picking up a snapdragon. Her eyes brightened. "I love this shade of pink. Do you think Mama might let me have pink walls in my new bedroom?"

Melody imagined sleeping inside a cloud of bubble gum. She wasn't sure she'd like it, or that Val's mother would. "I don't know," she answered. "What do you think?"

"Mama would probably let me have pink hair before she would let me have pink walls." Val started to laugh, and covered her mouth.

Just then, the piano music stopped. Big Momma called to them from the front of the house: "Melody, you have company."

Melody and Val exchanged puzzled glances.

"Company?" Melody repeated.

Filled with curiosity, both girls hurried to push through the swinging door and cross the dining room.

"Miss Dorothy!" Melody said happily. Miss Dorothy was sitting on the sofa, and Diane looked on from the piano bench.

Big Momma introduced Val.

"Welcome to Detroit," Miss Dorothy said to Val. Then she turned to Melody. "I've heard that you have selected a song for Youth Day—quite a special song."

"How did you know?" Melody asked. She looked at her grandmother. They had agreed that Melody would tell Miss Dorothy about her song choice, but she hadn't done so yet.

Big Momma shook her head. She didn't know either.

"I did it," Diane said in her bossy, too-loud voice. "I told Miss Dorothy."

"You?" Melody stared at her hard. "Why?"

Diane squirmed uncomfortably for a moment. "I wanted Miss Dorothy to know how good you might be! I mean, I was surprised at how good you were. I mean—"

"Melody," Miss Dorothy said, "I'd like to hear

you sing. I know that you've been working with your grandmother, and I expect you're doing quite well."

Melody was a little bit irritated at Diane for saying something to Miss Dorothy, but she was also flattered that Diane had told their choir director that she was good. "All right," Melody agreed.

Diane and Val went to sit beside Miss Dorothy. Big Momma took Diane's place on the bench, and Melody stood beside the piano. She wasn't a bit nervous—after all, she'd been singing in this very same room beside this very same piano for as long as she could remember. And she'd been practicing "Lift Every Voice" at home every day. She was ready to sing.

> *Lift every voice and sing,*
> *Till earth and heaven ring,*
> *Ring with the harmonies of liberty.*

The words and their meaning flowed out of Melody with confidence.

When Melody finished, everyone clapped. "Oh, very nice!" Miss Dorothy said. "Diane was right. You do sing this song well." Miss Dorothy looked at Big

Momma. "You have a good teacher."

Big Momma laughed. "Girls, how about some lemonade? Dorothy, will you have a glass?"

"Thank you, but I must be going," Miss Dorothy answered. "Girls, I'll see you back at choir practice in September. Valerie, I hope you'll think about joining our group."

Val smiled. "I'll ask my mama!"

While Big Momma walked Miss Dorothy to the door, Diane followed Val and Melody to the kitchen. Melody took three glasses out of the cupboard and filled them with ice. Val poured the lemonade. The girls sat down at the table.

Diane looked at the ice cubes in her glass. "I'm sorry I told Miss Dorothy about your song," she finally blurted out. "My mother and I saw her at the grocery store yesterday, and I just sort of said something. I couldn't help it! I never would have picked such an important song." Diane paused and looked at Melody. "I would have picked something . . . safe."

Melody looked at Diane as if she was seeing her for the first time. "You're saying you would have been *scared* to try this song?"

Diane took a sip of her lemonade. "I only like to do what I'm good at. You're braver than I am."

"But you're always so confident," Melody said. "You're such a good singer! You're always singing solos at church."

"Why do you think Miss Dorothy picked you to do the Youth Day solo?" Diane asked. "It's because *you're* such a good singer!"

"Maybe it's possible that you're *both* good singers!" Val interrupted. There was a pause, and the three girls looked at one another. They burst out laughing.

"Okay," Diane said.

"You're right," Melody agreed.

Diane emptied her glass and stood up. "I have to go. I'll see you both next week?" she asked shyly.

"Yes!" Melody and Val answered together.

After Diane left, Val turned to Melody. "You were right," she said.

"About what?" Melody asked.

Val smiled. "About Diane. She *is* getting better."

Just then, Big Momma swung the kitchen door open. "How's my chick?" she asked.

"I feel—brave," Melody said.

Never Give Up

♪ CHAPTER 14 ♪

Hot August came, and Sharon came home with it. She called Melody, and it was so unusual to hear Yvonne yell "Dee-Dee! Sharon's on the phone!" that Melody almost didn't understand what her sister meant. Melody was in her room, practicing her song with the tape recording Big Momma had given her. Melody ran down to the kitchen, and Yvonne handed her the telephone receiver. "Sharon?" Melody asked in disbelief.

"Hi! Did you miss me? We got back last night. My mother said I could come over this afternoon. I brought you some praline candy and a postcard."

Melody laughed. "Aren't you supposed to mail those things?"

"What? Pralines? I couldn't find any stamps," Sharon joked. "Have you been doing anything fun?

Did you decide on your solo for Youth Day?"

"Yes, and I'll tell you all about it. Val's been helping me, but I'm glad you're back. Choir practice starts next week."

"I know. I can't wait to hear you!"

"And I can't wait to see you. I'll be at my grandparents' this afternoon. Come over to their house after lunch."

"Okay," Sharon said. "See you later."

Melody hung up. She'd forgotten to tell Sharon that she and Diane had sort of become friends. "Vonnie, do you think Sharon will be mad that Diane and I are singing friends now?"

Yvonne was opening a bottle of mustard, and Melody noticed that she was making sandwiches—lots of them. Everything was spread across the kitchen table. "What?" Yvonne asked, as if she had only been half listening.

"Never mind," Melody said. "Who are all these sandwiches for?"

"They're for the group taking the bus trip down to D.C.," Yvonne said. "We're leaving tonight, and everybody's bringing food to share. Want to help wrap the sandwiches in wax paper?"

Melody nodded. "Are you excited about the march?" Yvonne was going to another freedom march, but this one was in Washington, D.C.

"Yes, I am!" Yvonne's Afro crown was tied back by a scarf, so that it was more of an Afro puff at the back of her head. Her earrings dangled as she nodded. "Especially after what happened to Charles and Tish. Nobody has the right to tell you where you can and can't live! If we had open housing laws everywhere, that real estate guy couldn't have done what he did."

Melody sort of understood. "But how is marching in Washington going to help them get a house in Detroit?"

"Hopefully there will be thousands of people at the march. A crowd that big will force government officials to listen to black people and change the laws all over the country."

"Will it be bigger than the freedom walk?"

Yvonne smiled. "Maybe. I bet all the TV news programs will cover it. Dr. King will be speaking, too."

Melody remembered how moved she'd been at the freedom walk, and how Dr. King's speech had helped her begin to understand "Lift Every Voice and Sing."

Melody stacked a wax-paper-wrapped square on top of four others. "And then you're going back to school," she sighed. "I can't believe the summer's almost over."

"Time goes fast when you're doing important work," Yvonne said, setting the stacks of sandwiches in the refrigerator. She put her hand on Melody's shoulder. "I'm sorry I won't be here for Youth Day. I expect you to write and tell me everything, okay?"

"I guess."

"I'll send you a postcard from D.C., all right? Now, will you come with me to the flower shop? Poppa needs as many hands as he can get today."

Frank's Flowers was as busy as a beehive when Melody and Yvonne arrived. Tomorrow was the grand opening of Tish's hair salon, and Poppa was making a dozen arrangements for her shop. He also had to do flowers for a wedding and a church program, and the store was full of customers. Gospel music filled the shop.

"Yvonne! You're late," Poppa said. "I need you to cover the phones and the cash register. Melody, go in back and help Val add greenery to the arrangements for Tish. And unroll that banner so I can check it before it goes out!"

Melody headed to the workroom. Val was sitting on a stool at the worktable, facing a row of small gold vases filled with daisies and red carnations. Lying on the table were bunches of ferns and pointy aspidistra leaves.

"I'm so glad you're here," Val said, shoving a bundle of spicy-smelling eucalyptus at Melody. "I don't know what to do with all these leaves!"

Melody smiled and climbed onto a stool. She tilted her head and turned one of the vases around to look at how the flowers were mixed together. Then she pulled a stem of eucalyptus, clipped it short, and eased it between two carnations.

"Wow," Val said. "Now it looks perfect. How do you do that?"

"I don't know." Melody shrugged happily. "Big Momma says everybody's got a way to shine. I guess arranging flowers is my light."

"You mean one of your lights. You've got plenty," Val said. Before Melody could argue, Val began to sing, *"This little light of mine."* She left Melody with the flowers and got down to unroll a long white banner across the floor.

"Look at this!" Val said, reading out loud: "Welcome to Tish's Touch of Beauty Hair Salon!"

Melody turned to see the large, glittery gold letters. *"Let it shine, let it shine, let it shiiiine!"* she sang.

"It's shiny, for sure," Poppa said as he came in to stand beside Val. "Are all the words spelled right?"

"Yes, sir," Val answered. "I know Mama will like it."

"Good," he said. "Let's box this all up and take it over there. She'll have time to get everything in place for tomorrow. You know how to take care of this, don't you, Little One?" he asked Melody.

"I know, Poppa!" She pulled two cardboard boxes and some old newspapers from underneath the work-table. Val watched as Melody put a couple of vases into the box and surrounded them with crushed newspaper so that they wouldn't bump into each other.

"Let me help," Val said, following Melody's lead. Soon they had both boxes neatly and safely filled.

Poppa rolled the banner up, tied it with a length of string, and tucked it into one of the boxes.

"I'll load the truck, and you two can go with me," he told them before he took one of the boxes outside.

"I'm so excited to see the salon," Melody said as she followed Poppa with the other box.

"Just wait until Girls' Day," Val said. When Melody looked confused, Val explained. "Mama always says that salons are for grown-ups, but right before special days, like Easter and Christmas, girls can come and get fancy hairdos and nail polish and stuff. It's lots of fun!"

Melody had never had her hair done at a salon before. Either Mommy, Yvonne, or Big Momma shampooed her hair at home. Then she sat for a long time underneath the noisy bubble-shaped hair dryer. Finally, Mommy or Yvonne would comb her hair out and braid it up. The whole process took all of a Saturday afternoon, and wasn't much fun at all.

When she followed Poppa and Val into Tish's Touch of Beauty Salon, she saw that getting her hair done in the salon would be quite different. Along the counter, there were three high chairs with footrests, all red. On the other side of the salon were two deep black sinks, and three big armchairs with hair dryers attached. Between the chairs were small tables piled with magazines, and mounted high on the back wall was a TV set. *It **would** be fun to get my hair done here,* Melody thought.

"Hey, what do y'all think?" Tish was cleaning the long mirror that stretched along one of the cheery yellow walls. She stopped and stood in the middle of the red-and-white-checked linoleum floor to wave her arms around.

"Looking good!" Poppa said, putting a box of flowers on the speckled red Formica counter.

"It'll look even better with the flowers. I like my place to be beautiful, so my customers start feeling beautiful when they walk in." Tish smiled proudly.

"This is so cool!" Melody said.

"These chairs go up and down!" Val explained, spinning one of the chairs with the footrest. Every time she pushed on a lever, the chair slowly cranked up.

"Be careful, baby," Tish said. "Why don't you girls put a vase on each of the tables for me?"

"And where do you want the banner?" Poppa asked.

"On the back wall," Tish said. "Let me get the stepladder."

Melody and Val finished quickly and then sat in the comfy chairs near the front window to watch the banner hanging.

"It's a little crooked," Melody said, squinting. Poppa pulled his end up.

"Now it's too low on your end, Mama." Val motioned with her hands.

"My goodness!" Tish raised her arms higher. "Tell me this is it!"

"That's it!" the girls shouted, giggling.

Tish clasped her hands and stared up at the banner. "Thank you so much for your help and advice," she said to Poppa. "At least this salon has gone the way we wanted."

"Remember the old song that goes, 'Trouble don't last always'? You and Charles are going to be fine," Poppa said.

"Looks like things are going to move more slowly than we planned when we came up here," Tish said. "So we'll be with you a little longer, and Valerie will go to the same junior high as Lila."

Melody was excited about the news that Val would still be living a few blocks away. That meant they could walk to school together. She grinned at her cousin, who looked pleased, too.

"That's all right," Poppa said. "We don't give up in this family, do we, girls?"

"No, sir," Val and Melody said, shaking their heads. At the exact same time, they said, "We make it work!"

When they finished at the salon, Poppa took Melody and Val back home, where they all had lunch with Big Momma. Melody was anxiously peeking through Big Momma's lace curtains at the front window when Sharon exploded around the corner and hopped up the steps. Melody pulled the door open before her friend's first knock. "Welcome back!" she said happily.

"Hey!" Sharon dangled a white paper bag in front of Melody's nose. "Pralines," she said, and then held up a second bag in her other hand. "I got some for Val, too. So, what's this amazing song you're doing?"

Melody was surprised. "Amazing? Who said?"

Sharon shrugged and walked into the living room. "I just heard, that's all."

Big Momma and Val were playing cards at the dining room table. "What did you hear?" Big Momma asked.

"Hello, Mrs. Porter. I was telling Melody that I heard the song she chose for Youth Day is amazing. My mother told me Diane's mother told her. But I still don't know what the song is."

"Diane's been helping me," Melody blurted out.

Sharon's eyes got wide. "Diane's been helping someone else work on a solo? Really?"

Melody didn't quite know how to explain to Sharon that she'd seen a different side of Diane—the Diane who struggled, even though she seemed confident. The Diane who was the same as they were.

"Diane knows how hard Melody's been working," Big Momma said, putting her cards down. "This hasn't been easy, but Melody isn't giving up. I think Diane respects that."

Sharon was silent for a moment, but then she grinned. "I guess a lot happened while I was gone this summer. So, what song are you going to sing?"

"Lift Every Voice and Sing," Melody said proudly.

"Melody didn't just learn the words," Val told

Sharon. "She learned what the words mean."

Sharon nodded. "I knew you would do something serious, Melody. Would you sing it now? I want to hear you."

Melody agreed, and Big Momma moved to the piano to play. As her grandmother began the introduction, Melody took a deep breath. She sang the song all the way through without any mistakes.

"Boy, you were *good*," Sharon said. "With our whole choir singing, and you leading? We're gonna turn Youth Day out!"

"Lila!" their mother called from the kitchen. "Have you got the television on?" Melody was already on the sofa with Val and her father. Daddy had stayed up after dinner on a work night especially to watch.

"Yes, Mom!" Lila was standing at the TV, turning channels.

"Stop there," Daddy said.

"Good evening," the announcer said. "Today, Wednesday, August 28, 1963, Washington, D.C. has seen what may be the largest gathering of peaceful civil rights marchers in the country's history."

Mommy hurried in and squeezed next to Melody, while Lila plopped down onto the rug. Everyone stared intently at the screen.

Melody could see a mass of people in front of a big white building with a row of columns along its front.

"Hey, that's the Lincoln Memorial!" Lila said.

The TV camera was way up high, as if it was in an airplane or something, so the people looked like thousands of tiny moving shapes.

"Oh, let's look for Yvonne," Val said, bouncing on the sofa.

"No way will we see her in that crowd," Daddy said.

The TV screen switched to a close-up of the marchers. The people were black, white, Asian, and other races, too. They were young and old. Then the screen showed Dr. Martin Luther King Jr., who was at the top of some high steps in front of them all. "I have a dream!" he was saying.

Melody's mouth dropped open. "He said that at the freedom walk!"

"Shhh!" Her mother patted her knee.

Melody listened, feeling trembly and strange inside. It was just as Yvonne had said. There weren't just a few families marching for fairness and justice, but so many people that a TV camera in an airplane couldn't get a picture of all of them at once!

"Will you look at that," Daddy said, smiling. "All kinds of people coming out for justice! This—this is history, girls. Our history."

Melody thought, *Surely someone will hear their voices this time.*

One Sunday

School began during the first week of September, and everyone settled into a new routine. Dwayne was still traveling with The Three Ravens, and Yvonne wouldn't be home from Tuskegee until Thanksgiving. Val walked to school with Melody, Lila, and Sharon every day. Lila had taken her school entrance test at the end of August. Even though she wouldn't know the results for a few weeks, she was much more relaxed and more fun now that the test was over.

Melody felt more and more confident about her Youth Day performance, too. Choir practice had begun again, and Miss Dorothy kept saying how pleased she was that the choir was working together. Now that Melody had gotten to know Diane better, Diane was being a lot nicer—both at school and in the choir.

On the third Sunday of September, Melody,
Lila, and Val sang together in the children's choir.
Afterward, Poppa and Big Momma stayed at church
for a meeting, but everyone else headed to their house
for dinner. The men were outside looking at Charles's
new car, and Mommy and Tish were talking in the
kitchen. Lila was upstairs reading. Melody and Val
had set the table with the yellow-checked cloth for the
family dinner, and then sat down in the living room
with a jigsaw puzzle. The only sounds were the low
buzz of their voices and the hum of the radio.

"It's too quiet around here," Melody said.

"I used to like the quiet," Val said, carefully fitting
a strange-looking piece into the puzzle. "But now I like
some noise."

"Oh, that's because you're getting used to all of
Big Momma's students coming and going around
here," Melody said. She tried to press a turtle-shaped
piece down. It didn't fit.

"And Poppa whistling in the morning," Val added.

"Mm-hmm." Melody turned the turtle piece a different way and squinted at the puzzle-sky.

Val pointed with her puzzle piece. "And you and

Lila and even Sharon are always running in and out!"

Melody suddenly saw where her piece slid in perfectly. "I knew it!" she said, looking up. "I mean, I knew you really liked a noisy, big family as much as I do."

Val smiled shyly. "I guess I do," she said.

But the noise they heard next they'd never heard before. It came from the kitchen.

"Oh, no! Oh, my goodness!" Mommy cried out.

"Lord!" Cousin Tish moaned.

Melody jumped at the sound, knocking the puzzle off the coffee table and breaking it apart. Outside, her father was yelling, asking what was wrong. The back door opened and slammed, opened and slammed as the men came inside.

"What do you think is going on?" Val whispered.

Melody heard her mother crying. Something terrible must have happened.

Lila came running down the stairs. "What is it?" she asked. When she saw the girls' faces, she asked again. "What?"

Mommy pushed open the kitchen door. Her eyes were red, and her face was wet with tears. Cousin Tish was right behind her, looking worried. She hurried past all of them to the phone. Daddy and Cousin Charles followed Mommy into the dining room.

Melody's stomach hurt. "Did something happen to Dwayne? Or Yvonne?"

"No, no." Mommy answered quickly. "But we heard terrible news on the radio from Alabama."

"What happened?" Lila asked.

"A church in Birmingham was bombed this morning," Mommy said.

Melody's tummy knot felt tighter. "Was it . . . was it the Russians?" she asked, confused. "Is it a war?" Mommy had said "bomb." Bombs were not by accident. At school they'd learned about countries like Russia making bombs and planning to use them against other countries, to prove they were strong.

"No, honey," Mommy said. "It's not that kind of war."

"Some people aren't happy about black people fighting for equal rights," Daddy explained. "They think bombing a church will scare us so much that we will stop marching and protesting and speaking up."

Charles looked at Tish. He was shaking his head.

"This is why we left Birmingham," he said.

Tish nodded. "There have been so many bombings."

Melody couldn't understand it. She knew that people disagreed all the time, even people in the same family, like Daddy and Dwayne. But a bomb!

"But what kind of people—I mean, how could anybody do that to a church?" Lila was still holding her open book. It was by Langston Hughes, and the title was *Laughing to Keep from Crying*.

"Did—did anybody . . . " Melody's throat felt tight. She couldn't get out the word that she wanted to say.

"I think lots of people must be hurt," her father said.

"Sunday school was in session." Her mother sank into one of the dining room chairs, as if she couldn't quite stand up anymore.

Melody walked slowly over to lean against her. Only a few hours ago she'd been in Sunday school herself.

Cousin Tish came to stand in the archway. She folded her arms around Val. "I can't get a soul on the phone," she said, her eyes wide with worry.

A car pulled into the driveway outside, and the sounds of Poppa and Big Momma filled the kitchen.

"Have mercy!" Big Momma came in with her church hat and her pocketbook in her hands. "Four little girls are gone! We heard on the radio in the car."

Val burst into tears, and Cousin Charles went over to her and Tish. Daddy rubbed Mommy's back.

"Gone? You mean—they died?" Melody pulled away from her mother. "At Sunday school?" Her knees felt suddenly shaky, and she sat down fast right on the floor, feeling as though she might throw up. She swallowed, and her tight throat hurt.

"This is insane!" Lila shouted, taking off her glasses to rub her eyes.

"It's evil." Daddy's voice shook in a way Melody had never heard before. When she looked up at him she saw that his eyes were red, and they flashed with anger.

"How can anyone have so much hatred that they'd harm children?" Cousin Tish whispered.

Melody balled her hands into fists, determined not to cry, determined to stop her insides from shaking. She couldn't stop either one. She wondered how old the four girls were. She wondered if their houses would be too quiet forever, because they weren't coming home.

In the kitchen, Poppa turned from one radio station

to another, but the news reports just kept saying the same thing over and over: "There's been a race bombing at the 16th Street Baptist Church in Birmingham, Alabama. The church is a meeting point for many civil rights activities. Four Negro girls were killed in the blast, and an unknown number were injured."

Charles switched on the TV, but it was too early for the news. Some sports show was on. Melody wished they would turn everything off. "Do we have to listen?" she asked.

"No, child, we don't," Big Momma said gently. She began to sing. Her voice was a contralto. It was rich and deep and now, sad.

> *There is a balm in Gilead,*
> > *to make the wounded whole.*
> *There is a balm in Gileud,*
> > *to heal the sin-sick soul.*

Melody knew the song. It was about healing. She closed her eyes, and then blinked them open, breathing hard. But she didn't sing.

Scary Stuff

*m*elody went home with her sister and parents in silence. Her head was spinning. Her stomach was spinning. Her throat felt as if it was throbbing open and closed. She had no more questions or words.

Lila went straight to the TV. "Oh, Daddy!" she called. "They're showing pictures of that church!"

Mommy went upstairs, and Daddy stood with Lila in front of the television. Melody didn't want to look. The telephone rang, and she hurried out of the room to answer it.

"Hello?" Melody sounded like she had a cold.

"Hello? Hello?" It was Dwayne!

Melody tried to clear her throat. "Dwayne, it's me! Are you—are you okay?"

"Yeah, yeah. We just played at Clark College in

Atlanta last night, and they put us up in the dorms. Man, the kids here are out of their minds over what happened in Birmingham. I can't believe it—a church on Sunday morning! That's some crazy, scary stuff. Listen, I just called to let Mom and Dad know I'm all right. My pay-phone money is gonna run out. Let me speak to Mom."

"Mommy, Dwayne is—" Melody tried to shout, but her voice was scratchy and faint.

"I've got it, Melody," Mommy called down. There was a click, and Mommy picked up the upstairs phone.

Melody hung up, relieved that her brother was all right. She passed Daddy and Lila, still watching the news.

"Going up so early, Melody?" Daddy asked without taking his eyes off the screen.

"Yes, Daddy," she said, hoping that he wouldn't notice her scratchy voice and tell Mommy to give her nasty medicine.

"All right, then."

Melody ran upstairs and curled up on her bed, staring at the poster from the Walk to Freedom. She stayed that way for a long time, long enough to hear the water running as Lila brushed her teeth, and Lila's bed squeaking when she lay down on it. Long enough to hear her parents murmuring to each other after Daddy came slowly up the stairs.

Melody tried to go to sleep, but sleep wouldn't come. *What were those little girls doing when the explosion happened? Laughing? Praying? Singing? What were their names?* Finally she must have closed her eyes, because when she opened them it was daylight again. Monday morning. Melody blinked at the Mickey Mouse clock.

"You okay?" Lila asked softly. "You tossed and turned all night."

Melody opened her mouth to speak, but instead of the words "I don't know," a strange croaking sound came out.

Lila stopped buttoning her blouse. "What's the matter with you?" Melody tried to answer, but croaked again. She put a hand to her throat.

"I'm going to tell Mommy," Lila said, rushing into the hall.

Mommy came in, half dressed for work.

"What is it, baby? What is it?"

Melody shook her head, trying to say something.

"With all that singing you've been doing, you may have laryngitis," Mommy said, smoothing Melody's hair. "I want you to stay home from rehearsal tonight."

Melody opened her mouth to protest, but Mommy put her finger to Melody's lips.

"There's another practice on Thursday. Let's see how you are then. I'll call Miss Dorothy. In the meantime, I think you should stay with Big Momma today. She'll take good care of you."

The next thing Melody knew, she was riding to her grandparents,' still in her pajamas. Val met them at the door, already dressed. Mommy and Big Momma whispered in the kitchen before Mommy came to kiss Melody on the forehead and slip out.

"What happened?" Val looked worried. She was wearing a white ribbon on her ponytail, and Melody remembered—it was Matching Monday. "Mama said you can't go to school today."

"My throat," Melody whispered. She really wanted to talk to Val about yesterday. Was she still upset, too? Had she been able to sleep last night? But Melody didn't get a chance. Tish came out of the kitchen wearing her salon smock.

"Let's go, baby," Tish said to Val. "I have an early customer."

Val slung her book bag over her shoulder. "Mama is driving me to school," she told Melody. "She says she doesn't want me walking for a while. She'll give you a ride too, tomorrow."

Melody nodded as Val and her mother left. Then the house was totally quiet.

Big Momma had put soft pillows on the sofa in the living room.

"Have a little of this," Big Momma said, placing a mug of lemony-smelling tea on a flower-shaped coaster at one end of the coffee table. Melody sipped some and then eased back onto the pillows. Her throat hurt a little when the sweet liquid trickled down.

"You just rest," Big Momma said. "I'm cancelling my lessons for today, so you can stay right here." Big Momma went upstairs, and Melody could hear her speaking in low tones on the phone.

Melody tried to get comfortable. She rolled onto her side, facing the piano. The heavy old upright was as tall as Melody was, with flowers carved into its music stand. The keys were no longer black and white, but had aged to a worn blackish-brown and tan. But Big Momma kept it tuned so that it played like it was new. Melody wondered if human voices could be tuned when they became worn.

"*Lift every voice and sing.*" She mouthed the words silently as she lay back on the sofa. Melody couldn't go on, even in her mind. What if she couldn't sing again? Youth Day was only a few weeks away. They were supposed to practice twice a week until then. She had to get better.

Charles stopped by during his lunch hour to bring Melody some special drops from the pharmacy for her throat.

"You just suck on these like candy," he said. "They'll melt in your mouth. Don't talk any more than you have to." Melody was glad she didn't have to say anything. She popped one of the rosy-colored lozenges into her mouth. It was warm and soothing and tasted like cherry.

For lunch, Big Momma gave her soup and brought her a brand-new book of paper dolls that she'd been saving for a birthday. Melody ate the soup, but couldn't concentrate on cutting out the paper dolls neatly. She rolled another cherry drop around in her mouth as her thoughts kept going back to Birmingham.

What did the four little girls look like? Were they dark brown, with skinny legs, like Sharon, and did they run so fast that their hair came undone? Were they tall and golden like Val, with ponytails that bounced and swung from side to side when they talked and waved their hands? Did they have sisters and brothers? The thought that something awful like this could happen to Melody's brother or sisters—or her cousin Val—shook her.

Melody heard Val come in the front door. It seemed like she was home much earlier than usual.

"Melody! Can you talk yet?" Val dropped her book bag with a thump near the TV.

Melody discovered that she could whisper. "How'd you get here so fast?"

"Sharon's mother picked us up. I got your home-work. School was so weird today! Nobody knew the girls in Alabama, but we were sad like we did."

Melody nodded and sat up straight. Suddenly she wanted to do something that would take her mind off all the sadness. "Let's go out," she whispered.

Val made a face. "In your pajamas? You'd better put on some of my clothes." Melody smiled, and realized that she hadn't smiled at all since yesterday. She borrowed a pair of Val's shorts and a shirt.

"What do you want to do outside?" Val asked, changing out of her school clothes.

"Plant," Melody whispered. Poppa had bought dozens of tulip and daffodil bulbs from the Eastern Market downtown over the summer. He and Melody had planned to plant them during the fall, before the frost. She knew that the bulbs would burst out of the ground in spring and bloom—the first flowers of the season. Poppa always reminded her that every season brought change.

In the yard, Melody felt like a mime she'd seen on TV. She used her hands to go through the motions, showing Val what to do and how.

"I got it!" Val said, digging with her spade just the way Melody did.

Melody wished she could use her voice to explain that thinking of new flowers blooming made her feel that the world didn't have to be ugly and bad, but could also be good, and beautiful.

Val held one of the dusty brown bulbs up to look at it closely. "It's hard to believe these things will grow into something pretty someday," she said.

Melody only nodded. She couldn't help thinking again of the girls who wouldn't grow up at all.

By Thursday, Melody's speaking voice was almost back to normal. Mommy had kept her home from school all week, so Melody had to beg her to let her go to choir practice.

"Do you think you will be able to sing?" Mommy asked in the car after supper.

"I hope so," Melody said.

Mommy drove up in front of the church. "You girls go on in. I'm going to find a spot to park and meet you inside." Val and Lila got out. As Melody slid across the backseat to follow, Mommy turned to her. "Did you bring the throat lozenges Charles gave you?"

"Yes, Mommy. But I don't think I'll need them," Melody said. Mommy seemed satisfied. Melody got out and closed the door. Then she started toward the wide stone steps leading up to the open doors.

The adult choir was clapping and singing, "*Oh, freedom! Oh, freedom! Oh, freedom over me.*"

Melody's steps slowed, and her heart beat faster. The voices were familiar. The song was familiar. Yet somehow each beat and each step went through her entire body. *Thump, thump.* She heard her own heartbeat loudly in her ears. At the top step she stopped.

"Hey!" Val's face popped around the door frame. "Why are you so slow?"

Melody couldn't answer, because she did not know.

The adults were finishing, and Miss Dorothy was coming toward her. "I'm glad you're here, but don't feel that you have to sing tonight," Miss Dorothy said.

Melody was mystified by the odd way she was feeling. Every one of her footsteps on the worn red carpet seemed to tingle. Her throat began to throb. Miss Dorothy was still talking, although she sounded farther and farther away.

"Melody?" Someone was calling her name. It was Mommy.

Melody blinked. Faces were crowded around her. She froze right in the middle of the center aisle.

"Melody!" Mommy shook her. Melody opened her mouth to answer. Nothing came out. Not a whisper, not a croak. Nothing. Suddenly Melody just had to get out. She wanted to be anywhere other than this church, any church! She jerked away from her mother and ran for the door.

"Dee-Dee!" Lila shouted.

"Melody!" Val called. "Come back!"

Melody ran outside, down the steps, and straight into Big Momma.

"Melody! Whatever is it?"

"It's her throat. She's lost her voice again!" Lila called from the door.

Big Momma took Melody's hand and started up the steps, but Melody shook her head hard, pulling away.

Her grandmother took one look at her and then called out to Lila. "You go on back inside," she said. "Tell your mother that I'm taking Melody home."

Big Momma raised Melody's chin with one of her strong hands, and looked hard into her eyes. Melody burst into tears.

"It's not only your throat that's hurting, is it? Something more is wrong," Big Momma said. "It's your heart that's hurting for those four little girls in Birmingham."

Melody nodded, still breathing hard, still feeling her heartbeats thumping.

"And you don't feel very good about going into the church right now."

Melody nodded again.

"I know. Honey, don't be afraid of the building. This is God's house. Everyone here loves you." Big Momma wrapped her arms around Melody. "Baby chick, I know it's hard to understand. Life is so special, so precious— and anyone who would take a life just doesn't hold love in his heart. Maybe there's no understanding it. But we have to stand up to the wrong of it. We have to keep our hearts and voices strong in the face of such a wrong."

Melody swallowed hard. How ever could she be strong, when she felt so bad?

Whispers

ig Momma told only Mommy and Daddy that Melody was afraid of the church.

Melody was embarrassed for anyone else to know, even Val. The idea that she might ruin Youth Day troubled Melody more than losing her voice did.

Instead of sending her to school on Friday, Mommy took Melody to the doctor. He looked into Melody's ears and looked down her throat and listened to her chest.

"I don't see anything that's really wrong," the doctor said. "There's no swelling in her throat. You say she's been rehearsing for a big singing performance?"

"Yes," Mommy said. She looked at Melody, but didn't say anything else to the doctor.

"She's not sick," the doctor insisted. He scratched his head. "Maybe it's stage fright," he said.

Melody looked at her mother. He was getting close to the truth without giving her any way to fix things. She wanted to leave.

"She's been singing in front of audiences since she was three," Mommy said.

"Well, then," the doctor said. "We'll just have to wait for her voice to come back on its own."

Melody pointed at a pad on the examining room counter. The doctor handed it to her with a pen.

What if it doesn't come back? she wrote.

"Oh, it will," the doctor said. "Sooner or later."

"Is there anything we can do?" Mommy asked.

"I suggest warm drinks and whatever else soothes her throat."

Melody hung her head. She'd been drinking tea and hot lemonade till she thought she might float away. She'd swallowed spoonfuls of honey, as Miss Dorothy suggested. She'd sucked so many of Charles's lozenges that she wasn't sure she liked cherry-flavored anything anymore.

The doctor peered over his glasses at Melody. "This must be a very special performance," he said. "Or a mighty special song."

Yes! Melody wanted to say. *I want to lift my voice and sing, but I can't! Now I'm letting everybody down.*

"Thank you, doctor," Mommy said as Melody hopped from the table.

Mommy tried to cheer Melody up in the car by telling her they'd have a big pancake breakfast on Sunday morning. Melody knew that was because they wouldn't be going to church.

Melody looked out the passenger window at the Detroit streets, where people were walking and talking and living their lives. A memory flashed in her mind of the TV screen, and the quick glimpse that she'd seen of smoking bricks. Nobody would be going to the 16th Street Baptist Church on Sunday. Melody shivered.

Would she ever be able to *not* remember?

Bo greeted her with a gentle nuzzle at her ankles, and then followed her like a shadow. Melody picked him up for a comforting cuddle.

Melody was surprised that Daddy was not only home from work when they got there, but he was awake, waiting just for her. He smelled like cinnamon when he gave her a hug.

"What did the doctor say?" Daddy asked.

"Wait for her voice to come back. Warm liquids," Mommy said.

Daddy smiled. "Well, how did I know that? I've got my all-time special Daddy cocoa with cinnamon sticks and whipped cream ready!"

Daddy only made cocoa when snow had fallen outside and everyone except Mommy had been out shoveling. Melody followed him to the kitchen, where she put Bo back on the floor. There was her favorite mug on the counter, waiting to be filled.

"You sit right there," Daddy said, tilting his head toward Melody's seat at the table. He poured the steaming cocoa into her mug without one spill. Melody leaned to sip around the puff of whipped cream and got a dollop on her nose, just as there was a knock on the back door. In came Poppa and Val.

Poppa was carrying a small basket of pink carnations, with sprigs of eucalyptus tucked at the edges. "How's our girl?" he asked, kissing the top of Melody's head. "Your cousin made this just for you."

Melody was beginning to feel uncomfortable with all the attention. She wasn't really sick. But she didn't feel well, either. Her voice was refusing to work. And despite what Big Momma had told her, she just wasn't sure that their church was safe. Couldn't hateful people choose any church to blow up?

Val held something that looked like a folded sheet of construction paper. "Sharon asked me to give this to you. Your class made you a get-well card," she explained, sitting down.

Melody pushed her mug to the side and opened the card. There were the names of almost everybody in her class, including her teacher. Big block letters said "GET WELL SOON." Next to Sharon's and Diane's names were drawings of small musical notes. Val had signed her name in one corner.

"I know I'm not in the same class as you, but I wanted to sign it, too," she said.

Melody mouthed the words "Thank you." She was feeling very tired. Not being able to talk was hard. Trying not to feel was harder.

"We're going to go," Poppa said, nodding to Val.

Val didn't seem to want to leave, but she got up anyway. "I'll come by tomorrow," she said.

When they were gone, Daddy picked Melody up, the same way he used to when she was tiny, and carried her to bed. "You have a big heart for such a little person," he whispered to her. "You take your time finding your way."

Melody wasn't sure what Daddy meant, but she rested her head against his chest, calmed by the steady beat of his heart.

Everyone tried to help Melody get her voice back and get her spirits up. On Saturday morning, she woke to hear the phone ringing. Lila was already up and out. Mickey Mouse was pointing to ten. Melody couldn't believe she'd slept so late.

"Melody! Telephone, in my room!" Mommy called.

Melody frowned as she got up. Mommy knew she couldn't speak. Why would she make her come to the phone?

Mommy and Daddy's room smelled like Mommy's fancy perfume. Melody always liked looking at all the pictures tucked into the frame of their dresser mirror and at Daddy's colorful ties hanging on the closet door. Mommy patted their blue-striped bedspread, handed Melody the blue telephone, and then slipped out of the room. Melody sat on the edge of the bed and put the receiver up to her ear.

"Dee-Dee, this is Vonnie. I know you can't talk. Just listen. I want you to know that the bombing in Birmingham won't stop us. Remember that lady who was afraid to vote? We went back this week, and she signed up. We've been singing 'Ain't Gonna Let Nobody Turn Me Around.' You know that one. Don't let anything turn *you* around. You've been working so hard on this song. The New Hope choir needs you. Don't be afraid to let your Dee-Dee light shine and shine and shine, you hear?"

Melody wanted so much to tell Yvonne that she *did* hear.

"Tap on the receiver if you get what I'm saying."

Melody tapped three times.

"Good!" Yvonne said. "I wish I could be there to hear you. You can do it! Love you. Bye!"

Melody sat for a minute after she hung up the phone. She was happy that her big sister hadn't forgotten her. If Yvonne believed in her, maybe she *could* go back to the church.

Mommy appeared. "Now, you get dressed, honey.

We're going to the salon."

Melody held both palms out as if she was asking a question, which she was.

Mommy laughed. "Why? You'll see!"

Tish's Touch of Beauty Salon was having a Girls' Day. When Melody pushed the door open, she saw all the girls from the children's choir, including Lila.

"Surprise!" Tish said, spinning a chair around. At the sound of her greeting, most of the girls turned to wave at Melody. There was Diane underneath a dryer, reading an *Ebony* magazine. She wasn't quite tall enough for her head to reach the dryer, so she was sitting atop two city telephone books. Sharon was getting shampooed. Some of the girls were getting their hair set on giant rollers, and one was having her nails painted. Some of the mothers were laughing and talking in the customer chairs by the front window.

"This is your seat, right here," Tish said, tapping the chair. Melody climbed in and Tish pumped the chair up so that when she turned it, Melody saw herself in the long mirror.

"Now, what kind of hair do we want for Youth Day?" Tish asked.

Melody shrugged in the mirror. *Will I even be at Youth Day?* she wondered.

"Hmm. Not sure?" Tish looked at Mommy. "I think the soloist deserves something a little special, a little fancy," Tish said. Melody saw Mommy raising her eyebrows.

"Fancy it is!" Tish said to Melody. "If you like what I do today, I'll do the same for you before the program." Then, as The Temptations crooned over the speakers, Tish combed out Melody's braids. She took her over to a shampoo sink. Melody wasn't tall enough either, so she sat on one fat telephone book.

"Now, lean back," Tish said. Melody closed her eyes. Tish's shampoo was so relaxing that Melody almost went to sleep. Tish wrapped Melody's hair in a towel and took her to a dryer right between Val and Diane. Tish took the towel off and lowered the helmet of the hair dryer over Melody's head. When she turned it on, the noise of the dryer blocked out all other sounds. For once, it didn't matter that Melody couldn't talk.

After her hair was dry, Tish straightened it with a hot-comb, and curled the ends up. When she spun the chair around for Melody to see the finished look, Melody gasped.

"She's talking!" Sharon shouted.

Melody shook her head. She still couldn't talk. She'd gasped because she looked completely different, like a more grown-up Melody. When she leaned toward the mirror for a closer look, she saw that her old self was still there. She was the same, but different. She was changed.

"So, you approve, Melody?" Tish asked.

Melody nodded.

"What do you think, Frances?" Tish turned the chair again.

Mommy looked long and hard.

"I think our baby girl isn't such a baby anymore," she said.

On Monday morning, Melody still couldn't talk, but she went back to school. She felt as if she'd been away for more than a week. Everything looked different.

When they got home, Lila opened the mailbox. "You got mail," she said, handing Melody a long plain envelope.

Melody didn't recognize the return address or the scratchy, cramped handwriting. She took the letter to her room and stretched across her bed to read it.

Dear Melody,

I bet you're shocked to know that your brother can write a whole page! Are you jazzed about taking over Youth Day? I heard you were having throat problems, but I'm sure that's all over now and you can't wait to sing your solo.

I am learning a whole lot about the music business, and not everything is roses like I first thought. We're just colored people on the road, like anybody else. Not even the big names can stay in the white hotels. Can you dig that? I mean, these guys have sold thousands of records, but they have to go in the back doors to perform in the top clubs! At the colleges, it's all right. But I thought talent would get more respect. Seems like our talent is colored first, and great second. I'm not

quitting, though. I love seeing how the
crowds enjoy my voice. I can't wait until I'm
*singing my **own** songs! I'm not letting any*
stupid laws or people with crazy ideas about
us hold me back. I know I'm good! You're
good, too . . . almost as good as me. Ha, Ha!
Best luck on your big day.

Your one and only brother-man,
Dwayne

Melody rolled over on her back and read the
letter again. Dwayne had been so sure that fairness
would come along with fame! It sounded like it hadn't.
At least not yet. She folded the letter carefully and
slipped it under her pillow. Melody remembered her
father saying something about the men he knew who
had given up when the music business got hard. But
Dwayne wasn't giving up. She decided she wouldn't
give up, either.

Melody turned on the tape recorder to listen to her
song again. She pictured Dwayne in front of the college
crowds. When she opened her mouth to sing, the words
came out!

Melody jumped up. She started the tape over, and she sang the entire first verse. Her voice was a bit squeaky, but she wasn't whispering.

"Dee-Dee!" Lila stepped in from the hall. "You're singing again! How?"

"Dwayne," Melody said.

"This means you can practice! This means Youth Day might not be a disaster! I'm going to tell Mommy."

"No." Melody took a deep breath. "I will."

Voices Lifted

elody called Val and then Sharon. She even called Diane. They were all thrilled to hear Melody's voice.

"Can you really sing?" Sharon asked when Mommy dropped Melody, Val, and Lila in front of the church for choir practice that night.

"I think so," Melody said. She was starting to feel nervous again.

"Well, let's find out," Sharon said, waving them toward the church.

At the steps, Melody froze. She couldn't make herself move. Her insides shook, and the awful fear of the fifteenth of September came back.

"I—I can't!" She looked at Val.

"Maybe if you just take one step at a time," Val suggested, taking Melody's hand.

"No. Don't make me." Melody pulled her hand away from her cousin's.

"I'll get Miss Dorothy," Lila said, sprinting up the steps.

Melody didn't care who they got—she could not, would not go in. If she did, she might be silenced again.

"What is it, exactly?" Val whispered. "Is it because you lost your voice in there?"

"It kind of looked like you ran into a force field from a cartoon," Sharon said. She and Val stared at Melody.

Melody wasn't sure what her friends would say if she told them the truth. She swallowed, half expecting her throat to close up again.

Mommy came around the corner from the parking lot at the same time Miss Dorothy came out of the church. They both hurried to where Melody stood at the bottom of the staircase.

"Melody, I'm happy you've recovered your voice. However . . . "

Melody sighed. "I know. You don't have to say it, Miss Dorothy. If I can't come into the church, I can't do the solo."

"Melody—" Val pulled at her. "Melody, don't give up!"

Miss Dorothy looked sad. "I'm afraid you're right, dear. If you can't do this, the choir will have to perform a song it already knows. And," she added, "I will have to choose a different soloist."

"We understand," her mother said. "Don't we, Melody?"

"Yes, Mommy."

Melody sat in the car while Lila and Val went into the church to rehearse. Melody needed time to think. She had to figure out what to do. Months ago, when Miss Dorothy had asked her to solo, she had been so proud! She had wanted to carry on her family's singing tradition. She had wanted to show Diane that she was good, in her own way. When she had finally picked her song, she had wanted to understand what Mr. Johnson was trying to tell the world with his words.

Then the church in Birmingham was bombed, and those girls died. Her voice had died with them, and now she was afraid of a place that had meant so much to her.

Melody remembered Yvonne's words: *Don't let anything turn you around*. When rehearsal was over and everyone got into the car, Melody leaned over and whispered into her cousin's ear, "I need help."

Val's ponytail bobbed in the darkness. "What can I do?" she whispered back.

"Let's meet with Sharon and Diane after school tomorrow," Melody said.

"I can't go into the church because I'm scared," Melody said, looking around Big Momma's kitchen table. "I can't figure out how not to be."

Val passed out sugar cookies and napkins.

"But what are you scared of, in our church?" Sharon asked, munching a cookie.

Diane was frowning with her elbows on the table. "It's not anything in our church," she said, looking steadily at Melody. "It's what happened to the girls in church in Birmingham, right?"

"Right," Melody said. There, it was out. Nobody looked at her funny. Nobody said she was weird.

"That scared *everybody*, Melody. Even grown-ups," Val said.

"I still have bad dreams about it," Sharon said.

"You do?" Melody was surprised. "You never said
so!" Melody had thought she was the only one who
was having bad dreams.

"You never asked," Sharon said. "You never talked
about that at all."

"Did you all talk about it?" Melody asked.

"Sure," Diane said. "At school. Last week, when you
weren't there."

Val put her hand on Melody's arm. "But we're talking now," she said gently.

"I know you worked hard on that song," Diane
said. "We've all worked hard, helping one another. We
won't let you down, and you can't let us down."

Melody tugged at one of her braids. "But what
if I lose my voice again? What if I think about the
Birmingham girls and—"

"We'll all go inside together," Sharon said. "You
don't have to be scared."

"*We're* four little girls," Val pointed out.

Melody nodded. She felt stronger, now that she
wasn't hiding her fear. Maybe she could do this for the
four girls who would never speak again. She could lift
her voice and sing, just for them.

On the first Saturday of October, Melody stood in
the midst of the excited young people gathering outside
New Hope Baptist Church. Buses were pulled up to the
curb, and cars were dropping people off. There were
children's choirs in neat white shirts and dark skirts
and pants; there were youth choirs wearing flashy
robes and sashes. Churches from all over Detroit were
represented.

"There you are!" Val elbowed her way into a space
very near the steps.

"I'm nervous," Melody sighed. Their plan had
worked for the last three practices. All the girls had met
out front and walked into the church together. Today,
that seemed impossible. The steps were crowded, and
groups of people blocked the front doors. Melody felt
a twinge of worry. Miss Dorothy had told them to be
prompt, and now they had only five minutes before
they'd be late.

"Let me through!" Lila said, pushing her way
past two tall boys, pulling Sharon and Diane along
with her. "My goodness! This crowd is huge! You
all had better get in there now, if you're doing that

hand-holding thing." She gave Melody's headband one tug to straighten it, and disappeared.

"Wow!" Diane said. "This looks like the biggest Youth Day showing ever!"

"Mmmm." Melody took a deep breath. "Can we just go in?"

The girls clasped each other's hands tightly and spread out side by side on one step.

"Ready?" Sharon asked.

"Ready!" the others practically shouted, and started to march up the church steps. Halfway up, two older ladies cut into the group, separating Melody and Diane from the others. Melody felt her hand dangle free, but she kept going. In the vestibule, Diane was suddenly gone.

Melody was alone at the edge of the center aisle. Her heart fluttered, and she swallowed. Miss Dorothy was already up front when she glanced up and saw Melody. Melody stood still. People were surging around her. It was no use trying to find the other girls again—she had to get to the choir. She started walking. The organist was playing softly, and the sound echoed all around Melody as she moved.

I have to do this, she told herself. *For the girls who can't go to church.* Melody locked eyes with Miss Dorothy and kept stepping. Val appeared from somewhere when Melody was halfway up the aisle, grabbing her hand. Then Sharon took the one on the other side.

When they made it to the front, Melody was trembling. She took her seat in the first row. Diane rushed up, breathless. Lila leaned out to smile and give Melody an "okay" sign. Melody couldn't smile yet.

After Pastor Daniels welcomed everyone, Miss Dorothy stood with her baton. The choir rose and took their places across the front of the church.

Melody stepped forward as the introduction began. In a move she did not expect, her three friends stepped forward, too. Melody wanted to say something to thank them, but she couldn't. It was her time to sing.

> *Lift every voice and sing,*
> *Till earth and heaven ring,*
> *Ring with the harmonies of liberty;*
> *Let our rejoicing rise,*
> *High as the list'ning skies,*
> > *Let it resound loud as the rolling sea.*

Then the chorus joined her, and it sounded as if Miss Dorothy's piano and their voices were doing a kind of dance.

> *Sing a song full of the faith*
> *that the dark past has taught us,*
> *Sing a song full of the hope*
> *that the present has brought us;*
> *Facing the rising sun of our new day begun,*
> *Let us march on till victory is won.*

The four girls held tightly to each other's hands. The audience clapped, and cheered, and stomped. It was no ordinary sound. Melody was overwhelmed by it, and also by the truth of the words they'd just sung. She tried to scan the packed room for her parents, or for Val's parents, but she couldn't find them. Then she looked to the place where Big Momma had been sitting, but she wasn't there anymore.

Dwayne was. He was wearing a black suit and a purple shirt and tie. He was clapping and cheering.

Melody felt faith, and hope, and rejoicing all at once.

When there was a break in the program, Melody rushed out into the congregation and threw her arms around her brother. "Dwayne!" she cried. "You came!"

"I wouldn't miss this for the world, Dee-Dee. You were fantastic!"

Melody stood back to look into his eyes. "Really?"

Dwayne nodded and draped an arm around her shoulders. "No kidding, kid. I knew nothing could keep you quiet for long. I just want to ask you, now that you're famous and everything—"

"—Dwayne!"

"You think you might find time to work a little with me, maybe do some backup singing when I cut my first record in a few months?"

Melody stared at him, wide-eyed. "You mean it?"

"Of course! But let's keep it between you and me for now." Dwayne craned his neck as he searched the crowd for the rest of the family. "I see Big Momma's hat feathers," he said, taking Melody's hand. "Let's go."

Melody felt herself grinning as she followed her brother. She had regained her voice, and it had been the hardest, scariest experience she'd ever had. Now she knew she would never stop speaking out for what was right. Melody Ellison would never, ever stop singing.

INSIDE Melody's World

The 1960s were an important decade for the civil rights movement in America—and Detroit was an important city. The automobile industry employed thousands of African Americans. Detroit's black community thrived, with its own cultural, economic, political, and religious establishments. Detroit was home to some of the country's first African American theater companies, publishing houses, radio stations, and history museums. In 1963, activists formed the Freedom Now Party, the first all-black political party in the United States.

When Melody's story takes place, Detroit had more independent black-owned businesses than any other city in the United States. The most well known was Motown Records, which was founded in 1959. The "Motown Sound" quickly became famous and influenced music and culture all over the world. People of all races listened to and loved the music that was born in Detroit.

While many African Americans had good lives in Detroit, they still experienced segregation and discrimination. There were no "White Only" signs on businesses, but African Americans could be refused service in stores, restaurants, and even hospitals. Black children went to separate schools, which often had fewer supplies than schools for white children. And as Melody's cousins discovered, some black people were not allowed to buy homes in neighborhoods that were mainly white. African Americans often had to pay more for housing, even though those homes and apartments were frequently in disrepair. This sort of discrimination existed all across America. The struggle for civil rights was not just a Southern issue.

Throughout the country, people spoke up about and fought for equal rights for black people. Activism was an important part of Detroit's culture. The city had the largest chapter of the National Association for the Advancement of Colored People, or NAACP. There was an NAACP Youth Council, and high school students and children as young as Melody were involved. Before the historic March on Washington, Detroit hosted the Walk to Freedom to support civil rights struggles in the South and to call attention to the inequalities that existed in the North. With a crowd of more than 125,000 people, it was the largest civil rights demonstration in America up to that point. Dr. Martin Luther King Jr. attended the event and debuted his now-famous "I have a dream" speech.

Although the civil rights movement had several key leaders, it existed because of the hundreds of thousands of ordinary citizens who played a role, however small. Children like Melody made a difference. They attended marches, participated in boycotts, and even spent time in jail. They lifted their voices in protest of inequality and in praise of social justice.

Read more of MELODY'S stories,
available from booksellers and at *americangirl.com*

♪ *Classics* ♪
Melody's classic series, now in two volumes:

Volume 1:
No Ordinary Sound
Melody can't wait to sing her first solo at church. She spends the summer practicing the perfect song—and helping her brother become a Motown singer. When an unimaginable tragedy leaves her silent, Melody has to find her voice.

Volume 2:
Never Stop Singing
Now that her brother is singing for Motown, Melody gets to visit a real recording studio. She also starts a children's block club. Melody is determined to help her neighborhood bloom— and make her community stronger.

♪ *Journey in Time* ♪
Travel back in time—and spend a few days with Melody!

Music in My Heart
Step into Melody's world of the 1960s! Volunteer with a civil rights group and meet Rosa Parks, sing backup in the Motown recording studio, or take a trip to Canada for the Emancipation Celebration. Choose your own path through this multiple-ending story.

♫ A Sneak Peek at ♫

Never Stop Singing

A Melody Classic

Volume 2

Melody's adventures continue in the
second volume of her classic stories.

rom the backseat of her grandfather's tan Ford Falcon, Melody read the big green sign at the side of the highway out loud: "Welcome to Alabama."

"We're going to pass Birmingham and go straight to the farm," Poppa told the girls. "I want to see it today, before nightfall."

Melody's knees were stiff from sitting in the car so long, but she could tell from her grandfather's voice that it wasn't a good idea to ask questions. She exchanged glances with Val, who gave her the zipped-lip sign.

The music on the radio was country-western, and Melody enjoyed listening to the way the lyrics and instruments sounded so different from the Motown music she listened to at home. Poppa often played country-western music while he worked in his flower shop, so Melody recognized many of the songs. She and Val sang along to the ones they knew, and they learned new ones as Poppa drove and drove.

When Poppa turned off the paved highway onto a dirt road, Melody thought they were almost at the farm. But Poppa drove for another hour to an out-of-the-way place, where he suddenly stopped the car. Melody's mother and grandfather got out and walked ahead into a field of slightly overgrown grass.

"This looks like nowhere," Val whispered, not getting out of the car right away.

Melody nodded and stretched, and then stumbled out to follow the adults.

Although she'd never been here before, there was something Melody liked—maybe it was the wildflowers dotting the field with shades of yellow and bright blue.

"It's hotter here than Birmingham!" Val said, pulling on a sun hat.

"Poppa?" Melody started after the adults. "When will we get to your old farm?" she asked, shading her eyes from the blazing sun.

Her grandfather didn't answer. He'd stopped to stare off at something Melody and Val couldn't see. Melody's mother turned to them.

"This is it," she said. "This is the farm."

Melody looked around in surprise. There was no orchard, there was no beautiful flower garden surrounded by a wooden fence Poppa had built himself.

All she could see were a few old trees and a dusty path cutting through the grass. In fact, nothing here was the way her grandparents had described the farm they had loved but had left years ago to move to Detroit.

"Poppa?" Melody said softly, tugging on her grandfather's sleeve. "Where is it?"

Poppa tapped his chest, and when he spoke, his voice sounded hoarse. "In here," he said, patting his heart. Then he bent to scoop up a little of the dirt. "And here," he said, letting the dirt run through his fingers back to the ground.

"You're standing on it. Standing on the shoulders of all our people who came before."

Melody looked down at her dusty sandals, imagining her grandfather as a boy, and his parents, and maybe even their parents, walking on this same path. She looked up at Poppa, and tried to stand just a little bit taller than she had before.

About the Author

DENISE LEWIS PATRICK grew up in
the town of Natchitoches, Louisiana. Lots
of relatives lived nearby, so there was
always someone watching out for her and
always someone to play with. Every week,
Denise and her brother went to the library,
where she would read and dream in the
children's room overlooking a wonderful
river. She wrote and illustrated her first
book when she was ten—she glued yellow
cloth to cardboard for the cover and sewed
the pages together on her mom's sewing
machine. Today, Denise lives in New Jersey,
but she loves returning to her hometown
and taking her four sons to all the places
she enjoyed as a child.

Advisory Board

*American Girl extends its deepest appreciation
to the advisory board that authenticated Melody's stories.*

Julian Bond
Chairman Emeritus, NAACP Board of Directors, and founding
member of Student Nonviolent Coordinating Committee (SNCC)

Rebecca de Schweinitz
Associate Professor of History, Brigham Young University,
and author of *If We Could Change the World: Young People and
America's Long Struggle for Racial Equality* (Chapel Hill:
University of North Carolina Press, 2009)

Gloria House
Director and Professor Emerita, African and African American
Studies, University of Michigan–Dearborn, and SNCC Field
Secretary, Lowndes County, Alabama, 1963–1965

Juanita Moore
President and CEO of Charles H. Wright Museum of
African American History, Detroit, and founding executive director
of the National Civil Rights Museum, Memphis, Tennessee

Thomas J. Sugrue
Professor of History, New York University, and author of
*Sweet Land of Liberty: The Forgotten Struggle for Civil Rights
in the North* (Random House, 2008)

JoAnn Watson
Native of Detroit, ordained minister, and former
executive director of the Detroit NAACP